Bacchus Death Collective

Robert Shepyer

ISBN: 978-1-62420-427-2

Credits
Cover Artist: Design by Ms G
Editor: Sherry Derr-Wille

Dedication

To Los Angeles, God forbid you ever become New York

Part I
Induction

Chapter One
Number Nine's Necro-baptism
Number Seven – The Thief

"One must die by fire, one must die by frost, one must die by poison, one must die by hanging, one must die by drowning, one must die by eating, one must die by being eaten, one must die by lust, one must die by suicide, one must survive and all must live in praise of Bacchus."
Hersh, Number 1, Christ-Bacchus, God-child

How did I wind up here, behind this mask? I was wearing the same one that the rest of the boys were, it's face was that of a beautiful woman's with an ivy-sprig crown, blue eyes and a grinning, dragon-tooth smile. All the boys but Number Nine, the Musician, stood in a circle while the girls watched from the balcony. I looked up at Number Three, the Astrologer. She was speaking to her daughter, Number Eight, the Virgin, Number Ten, the Chef and Number Five, the Sommelier. Over the course of my travels, I learned to read lips, it would prove to be the one skill that made sure I'd get out of the temple alive.

"The full moon is in perigee. This only happens once every thirteen months," the Astrologer informed the Virgin, Chef, and Sommelier.

"They'll be driven mad..." the Chef added.

"As if they aren't already?" the Sommelier asked, rhetorically.

"The moon doesn't feed their lunacy. Their lunacy feeds the moon," the Astrologer finished.

Perhaps she was right, the temple drove Number Nine mad enough to take his own life. He had been a victim of his own tragic disposition, slitting his wrists that old-fashioned way. The boys had been waiting in a circle, shifting around in their uncomfortable dresses and masks, until finally Number Four, the Magician, dragged Number Nine's corpse into the center of the circle beside the ivory tub. The white tub was filled with deep red wine that suffused the temple with cigar-box vapors. The

2

Magician lifted Number Nine up to the tub's lip to sit.

"May his dreams and memories be chained to this realm that they not follow him beyond. Take a good look at him, he is without his senses, and so his soul shall remain, unable to witness the glory."

The Magician paused and let go of Number Nine's corpse until it simply keeled over, to the side, splashing into the tub of wine. Once the body had been submerged, we all walked over to the tub's side.

"Each of you dunk him three times as tribute to Bacchus," the Magician commanded.

In order of our numbers, we lifted Number Nine up by his hair and dunked him back into the wine three times. I was the last in line to do so and once I had finished, it was my duty to lift the corpse out of the tub and onto the floor. I didn't think I could do it alone but when I tried, I felt superhuman power exuding out of every muscle. I looked at the moon, shining down from the oculus in the ceiling, it seeped a strengthening soma from out its craterous pores. With one arm, I took Number Nine out of the tub and threw him on the floor like a ragdoll.

The four women stood up from their balcony seats and walked down to the floor, knowing they would soon be needed for cleanup.

"In tribute to Number Nine's music, Number One will be playing the flute."

Number One, the Hierophant, Bacchus incarnate, lifted up his mask to reveal that thirteen-year-old baby-face we've all come to worship. The Hierophant was a special boy with a sad story. His name was Hersh and he was a hermaphrodite. Cast away by the world as a freak, he found a circle of people who would worship him as a God. He lifted his mask up to reveal those beautiful, golden blonde curls, his androgynous face, and those crusty lips. He brought his flute up to those crusty lips and played for us the perfect soundtrack to the violence that would ensue.

"In praise of Bacchus, tear the body to pieces," the Magician commanded again.

All of us spared no time in grabbing a limb or piece of tissue and pulling with all our might. Bones would dislodge and break before his flesh just split apart under the tension. Limbs, fingers, joints, and knuckles were flying up off the body in a frenzy.

"Embrace your divine madness. Let the nymphs seize you. The prince of pandemonium bequeaths you. Bacchus. Dionysus. The twice born. The lord of souls. Son of Zeus. Son of Semele. God of demonic silence and breathtaking violence. God of the most blessed ecstasy and enraptured love. Whose spirit is elemental to all that is created and destroyed and belonging to the Earth. In the name of this God, our God, who's come to us in human form, embrace your divine madness and tear this sacrifice apart," the Magician preached with startling theatricality.

When our hands were too slippery with Number Nine's blood, we resorted to our teeth and like jackals, ripped through the carrion without daring to swallow. With too many pieces to count strewn around the room, Number Nine had been divided up into an irrational number.

That's when the Astrologer and Sommelier pushed forward a vat of the mad honey. We all took handfuls of the honey to eat and celebrate the ritual's end. The Chef came around with a knife, stripping as much of Number Nine's fat off his pieces as she could collect. All the rest of him, the Astrologer, the Sommelier, the Virgin and the Chef would gather up to dunk in the mad honey for preservation.

We all lifted our masks and became men again.

"What now?" the Chemist asked.

"We drink," the Banker smiled and turned to Number Five, the Sommelier.

"I made a special wine for us tonight," the Sommelier informed us.

"Made it?" I asked.

"That's right, Jesus. Necro-baptisms and full moon perigees don't happen every night. This occasion was too momentous for just any bottle," the Sommelier replied.

With ample time between now and drinks, this is a good opportunity to make introductions. Hersh has to be Number One. Hersh is God as child, the homunculus, like Christ and Bacchus, he is twice born and from the water. Number Two is a man of just as much importance, a man of great vision but still, just a man. Number Two is the Banker, Charles Gaiman. Yes, *that* Charles Gaiman, of Gaiman-Billings, the mega bank. Stricken from birth with a terrible case of Omphalos syndrome, he is the financer of wars, governments, revolutions, political movements on the left and right, and cults like ours. Drunk with power and empowered to drink, at his old age, wine is his one true love, after his wife, Number Three. Opal Gaiman, Number Three, the Astrologer, is Charles' pregnant wife. Behind every great man, is a great woman and this great, big, gluttonous lady is responsible for the mad beliefs that infected Mr. Gaiman and led him to conduct this decadent experiment in the first place. The Gaimans' first child, Scarlet, is Number Eight, the Virgin. I've never seen a more beautiful blonde in my life, but I dare not act upon my impulses and touch her. Not to skip over too many heads, Number Four is the Magician, Salerno De Palma. With his giant, muscular frame, Sal is Hersh's greatest confidant. He would die for Hersh and our cult, because we are his key to the magical realm he's spent his whole life learning about. Mindy Oliver, perhaps my favorite of us all, is Number Five, the Sommelier or Somm, for short. She's a republican dyke with barrel-loads of attitude and has been working directly under Gaiman for at least a decade. Number Six is the Chemist, John Rollins, a PhD paid to make our drugs. Then there's me, Number Seven, the Thief, a title I take no issue with. I came to this country illegally from Mexico to steal my freedom. I didn't come here to work, I came to here to explore, like Byron into Albania before the world had such rigid borders. I ventured through South and North America as a poet, my feet led by the ancestral memory of my grandfathers and a lyrical flow in my mind. I was on a quest to improve my potency for poetry. From the moment I stepped foot in America, I decided I would meet the man who owns this country and lo and behold, Mr. Gaiman found *me*. He took a deep affection and appreciation for my talents. As a skilled thief and lock-pick named Jesus Madrid, he saw the irony in including me in his collective. Number Nine was the Musician, Leroy Rich. Now, he's a bunch of honey coated pieces, stewing in the bitter goop. Number 10 Ten is the Chef, a transgender male to female. She was born Ingo Braun but reborn Inga. She hates us all, I'm sure of it. Why? Because we use honey for religious purposes and thus, get a pass to break our vow of veganism. That's us. That's Bacchus Death Collective. The BDC.

~ * ~

The boys were sitting around a table in the dining room. It's a beautifully decorated room with vines and ivy growing out of every crack and crevice and crawling up the legs of our marbled table. The only women allowed in our vicinity are first the Somm, to serve wine and second, the Chef, to serve dinner. The Somm approached first, carrying a bronze decanter that was sculpted into Hersh's face. She arrived at the table and introduced her wine.

"Tonight Bacchae, I made a special and ancient blend of what is known as a retsina. Modern wine cannot exceed a fourteen percent alcohol content but with this, the sky's the limit. It's more comparable to a tincture, really. I wanted to make sure we all forget about Number Nine as quickly and violently as possible. The base wine is a thick and tannic Saperavi vintage 2014, with grape resin. It was fermented by burial in the soil of a marani cellar in Georgia. The black plum smelling Saperavi's dry, peppery taste is complemented by blending in the mad honey and a pinch of sea water from the Mediterranean."

The Somm poured each of us a glass of the retsina. We all took a whiff and sip of the vulgarly stout drink. Many of us coughed out our severed taste buds. Hersh even gagged up a bit of vomit. After a few swigs, we discovered the delight in damaging ourselves.

"I taste sour cherry and black currant," the Chemist began.

"It's a warming wine," I continued.

"It's like sandpaper on my tongue, did you dip-in your rancid finger to stir this blend, you wretch?" the Banker asked the Somm, smacking his teasing crimson lips.

The Banker would always do this, offend the wine, torment the Somm, and silence the table. This was his show, no one but Hersh ever dared make a peep against him.

"No, sir. I used a metal stirrer and precise measurements. Do you not like it, sir?" the Somm asked with an undaunted discipline.

"Fetch me something I'm used to."

"I'll bring two bottles right away, sir," the Somm smiled and skittered off, away from the table.

In the awkward stillness that followed, the Banker just shook his head. "Can you fucking believe her?"

That's when Hersh hurled his retsina up all over the table. The Magician sprang up from his seat with a bowl and walked over to Hersh as if he was going to comfort the child. Instead, the Magician reached over and collected all Hersh's bilious red slop into his bowl.

"Mustn't lose a drop, sacred fluid...never know when I might need it for a ritual," the Magician then turned to Hersh. "Will you be spitting up anymore, Lord Bacchus?"

Hersh leaned over the bowl and spit out the debris lining his mouth before he waved the Magician away.

"Thank you, Lord Bacchus," the Magician said then returned to his seat.

The Somm returned with two bottles of wine for the Banker.

"What do we have here?" the Banker asked.

"Some Lubrusca from your own vineyard. 2001."

"Excellent, my favorite vintage. Grows just a few hours from here, up in the Fingerlakes."

"Interesting," I replied, feigning interest.

The Somm brought both bottles to the Banker and placed them before him.

"I won't be needing a glass," the Banker informed the Somm, who rolled her eyes at him. The Banker then continued, "What was that wine we baptized Number Nine in?"

"Standard Beaujolais. Something the Chef would cook with."

The Banker nodded then stood up from his seat.

"If you'd all excuse me, I'd like to drink my wine by myself."

The Banker then strode off, carrying both bottles of Gaiman Lubrusca.

Chapter Two
The God of Error and The Error of God
Number Two – The Banker

"Every man and every woman is a star. Yet, a hermaphrodite is something more. We are the universe manifest as flesh. Two brains witnessing the world simultaneously out of each eye. With the might of man and the wisdom of woman, I can lead you up the stairway and down the rabbit hole. For I am the stairway. I am the rabbit hole.
-Hersh, Number One, freak, orphaned deity

How does one accept a painful death for the sake of nothing more than a God? The answer is *amor fati*, love of fate...one must fall in love with their own fate. One must accept the fate *we* give them. They must love their suffering and inevitable death just as much as they love their mothers. That said, whatever is to become of me, I accept and love it, nonetheless.

Hic, hic, hic...
I can't stop hiccupping....
BRAAAA....
Or burping....
My Sommelier can't see me like this, drinking wine like water, straight from the bottle...it would give her a conniption. I stare up from my bottle at the portrait of my hero hanging in my quarters, Andre the Giant. Below his face is the word 'Obey', so I do. Andre once drank one hundred and fifty-six beers in one sitting. Another time, twelve bottles of wine just in a car ride. If only I could drink that much, for me, two bottles are enough. I have to get this drunk to enter another dimension and from that dimension I can receive all sorts of divine information. I usually forget the enlightening strokes that hit me when I drink but not this time. I'm holding my phone and with it, I will record my testament. I press record.

Hic, hic, hic...
And I speak.

"Bacchus Death Collective is a group of nine illuminated men and women, each possessing a different kind of psychic power. I have assembled us together to sacrifice ourselves to Bacchus and summon his wrath upon the world. There are many problems in this world, but all of them can be solved with submission to the God of delightful insanity.

BRAAAA...

The first problem created by Judeo-Christian-Western-Civilization that needs to be corrected is the uneven distribution of wealth. There are two ways of implementing this change, one is by introducing a unit of currency to replace the dollar. The second way is by changing our Western value system. If the rich are to maintain supremacy then the prevailing mental condition must be delightful insanity. Bacchic revels could provide the poor with the delight and complacency to keep them at bay.

BRAAAA...

Why do you think Constantine declared Christianity as the official religion of the Roman Empire? It was because under Roman polytheism, the poor became too unruly and Christianity was the perfect system to pacify them. Now, seventeen hundred years later, in the American empire, the opposite is true. The centuries are but seasons.

Hic, hic, hic...

Monotheism but specifically Christianity, has failed to provide a mythological base for its practitioners to live prosperously. Christianity is oppression. It is only in the reversal of Christian symbols that true progress is attained. Satan, for all his ill repute, is the ultimate symbol and instrument of liberty. I would argue America itself owes more to Satanism than Christian piety. Christ would certainly condemn the sons of liberty throwing English tea in the Boston river. Satanism is but one chapter in the books of cloven fiction, his teachers are Pan and Bacchus and it is them who are the model gods.

Hic, hic, hic...

Where the Christians maintained the egotistical assumption of the soul's inviolable status, our cult teaches we are all one with nature, neither below or above the vines, rocks, and animals. Monotheism made nature demonic and the Earth a prison. Take the serpent for example, once a symbol of resurrection for its shedding of skin, Judaism rebaptized the serpent into a symbol of temptation and evil. What's wrong with temptation, anyway? Man, and nature, must make amends before nature finds us intolerable.

BRAAAA...

In the same garden as the snake, lived Lilith, Adam's first wife, who is considered one of the most reviled characters in the Bible. Yet, Bacchus Death Collective considers her a goddess and the original feminist. Angry that she was not Adam's equal, Lilith refused to be beneath him during sex. As rebellion against God, she then cheated on Adam to reproduce with demons. Hatred of women is nothing new to Christianity, though. Jesus had to be born of a virgin, lest he have to pass through Mary's filth-canal. In the time of Goddesses, Mary would've been worshipped above Jesus for being able to conceive anything immaculately. Which of Jesus' miracles compares to that? Turning water into wine? Clearly, that story is just another bastardization of the true twice-born God, Bacchus. You see, to ease Greek and Roman civilians into Christianity, the church turned Bacchus into a saint.

Hic, hic, hic...

Christianity has fostered a male dominator model of society and so we value male ego over all. Gone are the goddesses that led civilization for millennia. Marriage and monogamy have suppressed women into a form of slavery. Bacchus Death Collective teaches that group sexual activity should be encouraged. Our orgies are just as sacramental as Christian masses and through them, my wife is pregnant with her second child.

BRAAAA...

Most simply put, Christianity shrinks the soul. It is our devotion to Bacchus that has made Wall Street and by association, America, prosper. Why do you think we erected a statue of the charging bull in Bowling Green? The bull is one of Bacchus' many forms. Economics is not the only place where Christianity has failed, the arts as well. Film, literature, painting, sculpture, these mediums have never been so obscure and irrelevant.

Hic, hic, hic...

These are the beliefs of Bacchus Death Collective and by reintroducing Bacchus to the world, perhaps we can restore it to the Earthly paradise it once was, rather than waiting for a heavenly paradise promised to us by liars. Bacchus will empower women, reconnect man to nature, dissolve the male ego, and bring about new voices in the arts. Together, we can make America insane."

I ended the recording and slid the phone back into my pocket. My two bottles were finished and I was craving for more. Steadily, I departed my other dimension and lost grip of enlightenment. I would have to re-listen to my words so as not to forget them tomorrow but first, I had to return to the dinner table for food.

Chapter Three
London Broil
Number Ten – The Chef

"To live and die in praise of Bacchus, one must become enslaved by desire. Without choosing, one must pursue every desire, fantasy, and motive. One must eat. One must drink. One must dance. One must laugh. One must fuck. And one must never ask why."
-Hersh, Number 1, Lord Bacchus, The Twice Born

It is just like men to be so hypocritical as to ingest wine filtered with fining agents made of animal products and honey while pretending they're still vegan. Men, males, are responsible for the majority of suffering through human history, be it against other men or animals. The sum total of that suffering is higher now than ever and do you know why? Two words, factory farming. *Where every day is pure holocaust.* That is why I joined Bacchus Death Collective...because they aim to punish mankind.

For tonight's dinner, I plan to serve a cream of broccoli soup with raw cashew cream, a mango kale salad, rye spaghetti with pumpkin, zucchini, and hazelnuts, and for desert, beet carrot cake with butternut lemon sauce and topped with macadamia nut cream. I begin by boiling the pasta and steaming the broccoli, pumpkin, and zucchini. As I slowly stir the rye pasta in the boiling water with a wooden spoon, I can't help but think about how wonderful it would be t*o be eaten.* To be chewed, gnawed at, ripped apart by jowls. I want to switch places with the innocent, see how they suffer, *suffer for them.* I want to be the sacrificial calf.

Mother cows cry for months if their calves are taken from them. It goes without question they feel, think, and love. Yet that doesn't stop mankind from creating a system of farming them that thrives on cruelty. The science of farming for meat progresses only to make the animals suffer more. The animals are genetically engineered, restricted in mobility, and fed unnatural diets until they can't even naturally reproduce. Where else could you find animals living together with no inkling to have sex? Auschwitz.

There's a reason diabetes is higher in minority communities, it's because America has perverted nutrition into a tool for social engineering and eugenics. America is the world's most obese nation, eating more meat at a smaller price than any culture in history. In addition, sixty percent of our diet is made up of processed foods with manipulated flavors exploiting our desires for fat, sugar, and salt. These foods are filled with preservatives that shorten the human shelf life.

The first thing these Nazis do is knock the cow out by shooting it with a stun-gun in the head. The cow can be fully conscious, unconscious, or dead when it arrives at the shackler, who hoists the animal up by a hind leg. The cow is now dangling in the air when a 'Sticker' slices the poor creature's neck to sever the carotid artery and jugular vein. Blood is now spewing out everywhere and the cow is taken to a bleed rail to be drained. Keep in mind, some cows are still alive and kicking at this point. Once all the blood is drained, the carcass is taken to a head-skinner for peeling. Then off to the leggers, who cut off the bottoms of the legs. And finally, the carcass is completely skinned and chopped up for your fucking fat mouths.

I stew the broccoli in the cashew cream in one pan and fry the pasta up with steamed pumpkin, zucchini, and raw macadamia nuts in another pan. Constantly tossing and mixing the pasta, the taste of the world's most perfect food floods my mouth. Can you guess what it is? You'd be surprised to hear it coming from me. *It's dairy.* Mother's milk. To a baby, its mother's milk is a comprehensive diet in a single product. Everything the infant needs resides in the mother's teat. In fact, the milk's nutritional content evolves as the baby grows. It even feeds helpful bacteria in the baby's colon so the bacteria can multiply and compete better against harmful bacteria. What this goes to show is women are inherently noble while men are hardwired wicked.

Women are goddesses made flesh. That realization inspired my transformation. I was born to Russian Jewish immigrants who moved to London and named me Ingo after my grandfather who died in the war. I killed Ingo and out from his ashes, came Inga, me. For years now, I have undergone hormone therapy, much like the animals who are being engineered for feeding. I have yet to have surgery so I am walking around with a penis between my legs but that's alright, because this male body has been possessed by a goddess.

With the pasta and soup done, I tossed together a quick salad with mangos, pecans, cranberries, and three greens, kale, arugula, and spinach. Green vegetables are the most essential part of any diet, as they are packed with omega 3 fats. The American diet used to be able to get Omega 3's out of their meat but when factory farms stopped feeding their animals greens in favor of corn and grains, that's when meat just became dead calories.

With dinner finished, I plated everything and brought the food out to the drunken men at the table. They paid me no attention or gratitude as they traded stories of their various sexual exploits before joining BDC. I made sure to silently fart while serving their food.

The world is bleeding out, slowly and severely, it will soon be drained of all its life force, like a cow dangling over the bleed-rail. Factory farming is just as bad for the animals as it is for your body or the environment. Men will look back at this moment in time and wish they'd lived differently, eating less meat and being more conscious. That is, unless the right woman comes along and changes things, and for what it's worth, I'm going to try.

Chapter Four
Wine for Swine
Number Five – The Sommelier

"Christ died for yours sins but Bacchus returned to make you sin. When one vanishes, the other appears. If Bacchus is reborn in me then Christ has died, again. With all the wars we've waged, animals we've killed, suffering we've mocked, Jesus Christ died of a broken heart."
-Hersh, Number One, Christ-Bacchus, Bacchus-Satan, Satan-Christ

It is said there are no great wines, just great bottles of wine, and for tonight's tasting I've assembled six. These chosen wines have been shipped here from around the world by special order so that these pigs, who masquerade their sty as a temple, can drink themselves stupid and make believe they will change the world. I've been Charles Gaiman's personal sommelier for ten years now. At the beginning of my employment, I had the greatest respect for him as a man, husband, father, and capitalist. He was a self-made, hard-working man, who understood the value of a dollar even when he could've been wiping his ass with hundreds every day. I don't know at what point he got into all this Greek and Roman God garbage, but ever since he did, he's been a different person. I could tell something changed when he started saying things completely out of his character, like the rich needed to take better care of the poor and America wasn't a noble country, guiltier than any Middle Eastern dictatorship. All this Marxist, moral relativist, post-modern lingo you'd expect from a teenage nitwit was coming out the mouth of the very man those teenagers wanted to strip of power.

Along with changes in his political attitudes, he simply lost his sense of decency. He used to say thank you, please, and you're welcome. He used to open doors for me, even though I was *his* servant. Now he's lost all respect for me or anyone else even though as a somm, I must demand respect. For you see, what I do is a performance in a sense, telling the wine's story, serving the wine, walking people through the proper way to drink and taste a wine. I show people the respect to serve them, I expect the same respect reciprocated so that my performance may go uninterrupted. I'm not here against my will but had the job description said anything about death cults, I may have reconsidered taking the offer all those years ago. The only reason I don't quit is because Charles pays better than any boss I've ever had.

The history of wine is the history of how left-wing virtues have failed the world. The grape itself requires just enough water to stay thirsty but keep growing. In this, the grape acts as a symbol for man, where if government gives man no room for personal growth and responsibility, that man will spoil. Like rain over a vineyard, government should be limited. Communism devastated the wine industry of Eastern Europe, where vineyards were seized by government thugs with no idea how to cultivate grapes. Conversely, low taxes are what made Australia one of the biggest wine power-houses in the world. The left, which always preaches globalism and the deconstruction of geographic authenticity, doesn't realize that multi-culturalism evolves into homogeny, and same-ness is the end of diversified winery, the end of culture. Where culture ends, tyranny begins. The European Union will continue taking their cultural identities for granted until you'll see mobs of sober radicals burning the vineyards down to ash. At that point, as always, the great United States will come to the rescue, just like we did during the European phylloxera epidemic that ruined vintages all over the continent. Their only salvation was American roots that had to be grafted to the European vines.

Of the six wines, I've chosen three whites to start and three reds to finish. I took the bottles out of the cellar, placed them on a silver tray, and pushed the tray out of the cellar and into the dining room, where dinner had just finished.

"*Ah, finally*...something to wash down the splinters and drab taste of cardboard in my mouth," Charles began as soon as I stepped into the dining room.

I arrived at the table, standing straight and suave, not a hair out of place.

"Evening, gents."

"Hello, Somm," the Thief greeted me.

"Good to see you, Somm," the Magician doubled down.

"That blend you made earlier was so delicious, I've been looking forward to what you have in store for us next, Somm," the Chemist smiled.

"Thank you, thank you, thank you, and thank you."

"Get on with it, I pay you to get me drunk, not bore me to tears."

I began with the whites, as is custom.

"As you wish, sir. Gentleman, to celebrate Number Nine's destruction, I thought it would be appropriate to assemble and serve various sweet wines to delight all your senses."

"Booooring," Charles interrupted.

I didn't break my smile or even flinch, it's my job to be as cool as ice.

"We will begin our tasting with a bottle of Riesling vintage 1940. If you'll take notice to the bottle..."

I lifted the bottle off the tray and raised it up for all to see its golden label with German words written below a red swastika emblazoned upon the storied glass.

"This bottle comes from the region of Alsace, which has changed hands between France and Germany for the last two hundred years. Soldiers stomped directly over vineyards to wage war. In 1940, it was under Nazi control."

Using an elegant thousand-dollar corkscrew, I opened the bottle and poured its contents into everyone's glasses.

"Don't let the Nazis' reputation fool you. They like their wine tasting sweet with hints of apples, apricots, and honey. That signature German ruthlessness you know so well, is hidden in the wine's scent where there is a rather sharp aroma of petrol and gasoline."

Everyone seemed happy tasting their wine and puckering their lips to its supple fruitiness with the exception of Charles.

"Something wrong, sir?"

"You know I was born Jewish, Somm."

"Yes, but you don't practice so I didn't see the harm."

"You're not a Jew, Charles. You're a Bacchae," the Magician injected to Hersh's delight.

"Bacchae or Jew, I have no interest in sampling this coward water you've given me. I like strong wines, Somm."

"What is the point of a sample if not experiencing new flavors and expanding your horizons?" I asked.

"My taste is vaster and with more depth than your pitiful soul,

Somm. I want what *I* like, not what *you* like."

"Please sir, talking's dry work, why let good booze go to waste?"

He grumbled at me then in one quickly motion, up down, snapped the liquid back into his mouth.

"I'm ready for the second bottle, Somm," Charles obnoxiously stated the moment his glass hit the table. Meanwhile, the others were still savoring the wine at the proper pace.

"Not till everyone's finished, sir," I replied.

"Are you talking back to me?" he fumed.

To avoid Charles' inevitable outburst, the rest of the men just finished their glasses right then.

"Looks like everyone's finished then...time to move on," I smiled.

I returned to my tray of bottles and picked up the second white. It was darker and sweeter than its predecessor.

"Your second glass will be Terrantez vintage 1960 from the island of Madeira, off the coast of Portugal."

With this wine, the Portuguese proved they could produce something decent, in their drug abusing, decadent, law-less country.

"The story of Madeira, the island that some believe is the lost city of Atlantis, can be told in the flavor of its wines. When the Portuguese arrived on the island in 1419, they set fire to the dense forests and left the soil enriched by its ash. Of this wine specifically, an old Portuguese proverb says "The grapes of Terrantez are not for eating, nor to give them away, but for wine, God created them."

"Is that true, Lord?" the Magician tuned to Hersh for appeasement.

Hersh shrugged then nodded, appeasing the Magician.

"There was a time these grapes were thought to be extinct and now even with Terrantez seeing a comeback, vintages like this one are incredibly rare and sought after."

"Just get on with it...*BRAAAA*...will you?" Charles shouted and burped, already buzzing.

I started pouring everyone a glass and was so spellbound by the wine's beautiful, mahogany color that no amount of offense from Charles could've phased me. It is moments like these that remind me why wine is my one true love. I couldn't wait to get this wine to myself when I got back into the cellar.

"The wine is white, medium dry, and very sweet. As per usual, I suggest you smell the wine first and let it access your memory banks."

Everyone brought their wine glasses up to their noses and closed their eyes to drift away in its image conjuring, deep aroma.

"What do you smell?" I asked the table.

"My nose tells me jasmine..." the Thief began.

I'd never admit it, but the Thief had a style I found almost irresistible. He had an air about him that was undeniably sexy.

"Yes. Jasmine. Most definitely. Now everyone taste," I instructed the men.

They elegantly swished the liquid in their glasses and took modest sips. Charles though, drank the whole glass in one ferocious guzzle.

"That's absolutely delicious...it tastes like caramel," the Thief exclaimed with an adorably devious smirk on his face.

"More like rotten grapes," Gaiman continued.

"I'm saving that for the next, actually...does anyone else feel the same way about the Terrantez?"

The Magician smacked his lips and spoke, "I get hazelnuts. I love hazelnuts," the Magician then finished his glass. "It's a great wine."

"*Oh really? IS IT?* Well, what a sophisticated palette you must have," Charles obnoxiously teased the Magician.

He then turned to me, "Give me the bottle, I need more to know for sure."

I passed Charles the wine, knowing full well no bottle leaves Charles' hands with any wine left in it. He sucked upon the rare bottle like a fish until all its contents were gone and doomed to amount to nothing more than an especially deep hued piss.

"I'm ready for my second bottle, Somm...*hic,*" Charles drunkenly slurred.

Hiding my sadness that I wouldn't be able to taste the Terrantez myself, I picked out the third and final white, another delicacy.

"Until 1949, Tokaj had been the greatest wine in all of Eastern Europe. It was a wine for noblemen and royalty. When the country became communist and winemaking was put in the hands of the state, the craft was homogenized and passion for making quality wine disappeared."

"Tell me you have a communist wine for us to sample..." Gaiman begged.

"No, I'm afraid not. It was only when the region began to privatize its wine industry and vineyards were returned to their rightful owners, that steps were taken to reclaim the country's rich liquid history."

I uncorked the golden bottle and began pouring all the men a glass.

"This wine's story is as bizarre as its method of cultivation. The region's cooler months are stricken with a moist dew that nobly rots the grapes with a gray mold called botrytis. The warmer months dry the grapes, making them shrivel, concentrating their sugar, acid, and flavor."

Everyone's glass was now full with the exception of Charles.

"It tastes of ginger and saffron."

I arrived at his side and tilted the bottle to pour in his glass but he quickly slapped the glass off the table and it shattered on the marble floor.

"I can no longer limit my thirst to a small orb. The new rule is that what doesn't get poured in their glasses goes directly down my throat," Charles growled as he tore the bottle out of my hands.

One day, it'll be hemlock in that bottle, I thought. *Though, I bet he'd see it coming and still drink it to the last drop.* ☺

Charles didn't wait to smell or observe the wine, like the last bottle, he just leaned his head back and got rid of it without any appreciation for the Hungarian plight it took to arrive into his filthy mitts. He smacked his lips, clearly deterred by the wine's sweetness and set the bottle down.

"Are you trying to kill me, Somm?" he said. with deadly seriousness.

"Why do you say that?"

"I think that syrup made me diabetic."

"If it did kill you then you'd have fulfilled the role of *the one that dies by poison*, thereby serving The Collective," Hersh spoke. His soft and timid voice held the power to freeze the whole room.

Charles stared at Hersh, too drunk to know which expression to project while Hersh kept his eyes down on the table, coldly.

"I realize that, Hersh... We're all here to give the Collective our lives. Until then, let us enjoy them, please," Charles rudely replied.

Antagonizing Hersh was heresy. Though no one made much of it past a few awkward, plotting glances, it had been stored in the minds of Hersh and the Magician; the Banker earned his death in royal spades.

From delicate, dry and sweet whites. It was now time to change the evening's direction into the red.

"Our crossing over from white to red will highlight the world's three most prominent regions of wine, those being France, Italy, and Spain. We'll begin with Spain."

I picked up the fourth bottle.

"This is a bottle of Cabernet Sauvignon from the region of Rioja, vintage 2012. It's the youngest wine you'll be drinking tonight but has the hardest kick. It's dense, concentrated, and abrasive. Its intense flavor has notes of licorice, herbs, and orange. A strong wine, Charles...just for you."

"You're too kind, Somm," Charles tilted his head, sarcastically.

Once I poured the Cab around and gave Charles his bottle, I returned to the head of the table to observe everyone's reactions.

"What do you think?"

"I feel sophisticated drinking this...thank you, Somm," Jesus said.

I nodded, politely.

"I enjoy it, too, it's a contemplative wine," the Magician followed.

"It's so good, I think you've earned a toast, Somm. You've done well," the Chemist raised his glass, as did everyone but Charles, and their voices married together for one hefty "*Thank you, Somm.*"

"It's like drinking lead," Charles exclaimed as he pulled the bottle away from his lips, half done.

"It's a disgusting wine, the choice to serve it was disgusting, and the person serving it is also disgusting," Charles smiled then brought the bottle back to his lips to polish it off.

"I don't care what you say about me, but do not insult the wines."

"Fuck your wine," Charles said, as he flung the bottle at my head. I ducked at just the right moment and the bottle crashed against the wall, exploding into shards of glass.

"*I can't do this,*" I whimpered.

He finally broke me. I could only take so much. With my eyes filled with tears and my constitution turned to rubble, I quickly ran from the table until Charles stood up from his seat.

"If you don't finish serving us the last two wines, then you will not make it out alive, Somm...*and that's a promise.*"

I stopped in my tracks, knowing he was serious and turned around. Swallowing my pride, I returned to the table and my wines. I introduced the fifth wine with tears streaming down my cheeks.

"Our fifth wine is an Italian Nebbiolo from the region of Barolo vintage 1996. The wine is highly tannic, smoky, and uncompromising with a rhapsody of flavors mingling within."

"*BRAAAA...*" Charles belched.

I shrugged off the interruption and continued, "You will taste raspberries, cherries, and roses but also leather, clay, and truffles."

I poured the wine all around and when I set the bottle down before Charles, he looked at me with what seemed like sympathy and with a finger, wiped away my tears.

"Thank you, sir," I acted like his touch was welcomed but nothing could be further from the truth.

Like a vampire, he took my tears from his finger and dropped them into the Nebbiolo. Staring at me, he drank the tear-infused wine, smiling as his mouth pursed around the bottle's lip. He finished without breaking his stare and put the bottle down to speak.

"This has to be my favorite wine of the evening."

"I'm happy you like it, sir."

I returned to the head of the table and watched everyone enjoy the wine. Once they finished, I picked up the final bottle.

"Our last bottle had to be French. No other country gives more praise to Bacchus. That's why the final bottle I chose is Hermitage vintage 1990. The story of hermitage is of a knight injured in the crusades. He returned home a war hero. For his service, the Queen of France rewarded him with the chance to recover on the hill of Hermitage in the Rhone Valley. The knight loved this place so much he never left and the villagers called him the hermit. Thus, the name, Hermitage. The wine is massive, rich and filled with fruity flavors. It is the perfect send-off to Number Nine because it is music made liquid."

I uncorked the bottle then poured it all around until arriving at Charles' side. I just stood before him and smiled.

"Well, what are you waiting for? Wipe that stupid...*hic*...smile off your face and give me my booze."

Casually, I raised the bottle and started drinking, doing my best impression of a hedonist, chugging the liquid down, my gullet throbbing with every gulp. This was heresy of the highest order, not just because I was taking wine away from a higher number, my boss, but because women were not allowed to drink in our cult. For as much feminism and deconstruction of the male ego as we preach, nothing is turned into practice. When I finished Charles' booze, I put the bottle down right below his nose.

"How was it?" he asked.

"No wine is worthier of symbolizing Christ's blood," I answered with additional heresy.

Charles' lips curled into a smile and almost laughed until he stood up and raised his fist over me. Before he could strike, Hersh jumped out of his seat and pulled Charles' arm back.

"What are you doing?" Hersh growled.

"She committed heresy against you, Lord," Gaiman explained.

"Then it is *MY* duty to punish her, not yours."

Charles turned around to face Hersh, retiring his hand down by his side.

"What are you going to do then?"

"Come to me, Number Five," Hersh commanded me.

I stepped around Charles and confronted the God-child chest to face.

"If you'd like to leave us, there's the door," Hersh pointed to the great white ivy-covered door.

"I don't want to go. I'm happy here," compared to the world out there, this wasn't all that bad.

"Are you sure? You might end up regretting this decision once the world changes into a place you no longer recognize. Now is your chance to return to it while it's still intact."

"I'm sure, Hersh."

"Then you will follow the law and refer to me as Lord, now and always."

"Yes, Lord."

"There will be no more of this Christ business. I suspect he had something to do with your compulsion to drink Number Two's wine."

"Perhaps."

"Ruminate on it. Now, is your tasting over?"

"Yes."

"Return to your quarters and don't come out unless summoned."

"Thank you, Lord."

Hersh simply nodded and after an awkward pause. I skittered away like a roach back into the shadows. Charles grabbed the empty bottle of Hermitage and raised it upside-down over his mouth. A single drop trickled down the inside of the bottle's side until reaching the lip and hanging off to loom over his gaping mouth. He shook the bottle only slightly and worked the drop off, making it land just beside his foot.

"Fuck... *hic*."

Charles kneeled down like a dog and lapped up the drop of wine from the floor. He raised his head with a smile on his face, looked around at all his fellow Bacchae and said, *"Damn, that's good stuff!"*

Chapter Five
The Ritual
Number Four - The Magician

"Humanity rehearses the same play throughout all time. Freedom fails us and corruption triumphs. Then language decays and tyranny ensues. Everything you know, believe, and see is a result of empiricism and opportunism"
-Hersh, Number One, Creator of Honey

Many days and nights passed since Number Nine had taken his life. In that time, we had been preparing the ritual of initiation. Upon the evening of the half-moon, everyone had gathered into the temple to watch me draw the circle. I had dusted off my black robes for the occasion.

"Why is it you're wearing a black robe instead of your usual white on this evening, Magician?" the Thief asked.

"The rule is waxing moon for benevolent magic, waning moon for malevolent magic. White for benevolent, black for malevolent," I answered.

On the last half-moon, I performed a ritual, wearing white robes, where I summoned the spirit of Bacchus and he entered Number One, Hersh, our Lord and Hierophant. That time and now in this ritual, a tub had been prepared with sea-water for Number One to lay in. Holding a bull's baculum, our Lord waited in the water for me to draw the circle.

"Are you ready, Lord?" I asked him.

He nodded with a pained and scared expression. The poor boy. Like Christ, this god was partly flesh, who's adolescent heart and mind were being torn apart by the pressures of his own divinity.

I began drawing the circle's outer rim to set its boundaries. I traced it with red paint infused with wine and soil from Beaujolais. On the inside of the circle, I painted the necessary symbols to appease Bacchus. The pentacle with each of its five points touching the rim, the Qabalistic Tree of Life in the pentacle's center, and the name Bacchus, written in Hebrew on the tree.

Now that the circle was painted, it was time to consecrate it. I required certain supplies from the Chef and Chemist. The Chef gave me sea-salt from the Dead Sea, Ceylon cinnamon from Sri Lanka, a mother of pearl vial of olive oil, and five candles made of Number Nine's fat. The Chemist gave me raw mercury and sulfur. I sprinkled the sea-salt and cinnamon around the circle's rim and spread the mercury and sulfur symbolically within the Qabalistic Tree of Life. Finally, I had placed each of the five candles at the pentacle's points and washed my head and hands in the olive oil so that Minerva may bless me with wisdom.

This ritual requires five men and since Number Nine was no longer with us, we had no choice but to include Inga, formerly Ingo, to stand at one point of the pentacle. I'm not sure what the effect of this compromise will be but I hope *his* psychological womanhood won't disrupt the ritual. Every man gathered and was standing in place. The half-moon glowed above us in glorious opulence. The alter was ready with the purple leather-bound book of conjurations, the dagger, and the brass goblet filled with fire. Hersh had been clutching his bull baculum tightly, flat against his sternum, as he lay submerging all but his mouth and nose in the tub's sea-water.

I began my mantra.

"My consciousness does not belong to me, your consciousness does not belong to you." Over and over, I repeated this until it warped into nonsense.

"My consciousness does not belong to me, your consciousness does not belong to you. My conschousess dos noh bilung toe mee; yo cohshous oes no long ta yew. Miconsho dono belotomi; urconsho dono lotoyu."

After that, the others began chanting the temple's mantra.

"Every man and woman is a star. Every man and woman is a star. Every man and woman is a star."

Surrounded by a wall of chanting, I stopped speaking and stepped over to the alter. I opened the book of conjurations to the page with the Summoner's Prayer, took the dagger and burning goblet in my hands. As the men chanted, I strolled around the circle pouring liquid fire from my goblet into each of their goblets. Once each goblet was burning, I stopped east of the alter, facing Number One and recited the Summoner's Prayer.

"Christ-Bacchus, the innocent babe,

Like the branch's olive or the vine's grape,
From Earth and water and heat you are born,
Not once but twice like the bull's horn,
East of the Alter I stand before you,
With Goblet and Dagger like a statue,
Holy Child, let thy name go undefiled,
Let thy name make mankind beguiled,
Thy time has come, thy will is done,
Now your blood like wine must run,
But before I cut you, please tell me when,
With a sign of wisdom, Amen."

The room fell deafly quiet and I closed my eyes, preparing to sacrifice my thoughts. Emptying my brain in solemn meditation, I took astral shape outside my body to commune with whatever angels my prayer baited. They act as guides, these angels, they always have. When Bacchus first entered Hersh, I saw my mother take an angel's form. A woman who went insane, the whore of Babylon reborn into flesh then renewed as an angel. She instructed me to make the first cut upon Hersh's head. Now, floating toward me from out of the darkness, I see the angel of my second ritual...with a bald head and stout stature, I know exactly who to expect...my father, the stone mason. Working hard to feed his kin, he was a man of simple thought. He appeared as an ascetic angel, in a linen robe with hammer in hand, a mason for all seasons.

"This temple is a house of sin and deception. This is not your fate, my child, nor is it Hersh's," my father said.

"Do you want me to cut him, Father?" I asked aloud.

"No. Do not harm the child."

I now had a dilemma on my hands. Ending the ritual without a summoning would spell the end of all our efforts. The world would remain flawed and I would be nothing more than the hapless Magician, son of a stone mason and a whore.

"As you wish, Father," I said aloud.

I opened my eyes to see Hersh before me, in the water and waiting for my dagger. As if my father instructed the opposite, I floated the blade over Hersh's head and ever so gently, I cut him just enough to break the skin. The moment the blade breached him, Hersh's mind erupted. Convulsing in the water, splashing out the candles around him, Hersh's interior darkness shot out of his mouth and eyes in the form of shadows shaped like black beams. These shadows screeched and howled, grabbing at whatever they could and charring the white marble walls. After Hersh expelled all his darkness, the shadows escaped out the oculus and went flying into Manhattan to run amuck, terrorizing the city. Poor Hersh had been drained so empty he lost consciousness and nearly drowned in the sea-water. I pulled him out of the tub and onto the floor and breathed air into his baby lungs. After a few hysterical moments, I was able to revive the child.

"Lord Bacchus, are you alright?"

He nodded, half-alive, still coughing out water.

"What did you see?" I asked.

"Light...."

"Praise you, Lord Bacchus."

I had no idea what I unleashed. It may turn out to be the change we were hoping for, the Bacchic revels that would bring mad delight back into this realm. It may also turn out to be this world's end, we won't know until it's too late. It was not until the next morning that Number Two informed us that on the previous evening, the mothers of New York all killed their first-born sons. The plagues of Egypt paid this new world a visit.

Chapter Six
Virgin Tears of a Crocodile
Number Eight – The Virgin

"Madness delights in restriction. Madness does not suffer the mad. Madness protects the mad from freedom."
-Hersh, Number One, the Mad God

My daddy doesn't want me using a phone but sometimes, if I'm a really good girl, he'll let me have his for an hour. I usually just take selfies and post them on Instagram. Even though they all look the same, seeing as I can't leave the temple, they still get plenty of likes just because I'm famous, ya know?

My Twitter newsfeed was bombarded by the fruits of our labors. After all the weird stuff that happened in the ritual, a lot of weirder stuff started happening in New York. Hundreds of women killed their oldest sons and for a few days, people had no idea what to make of it. Zombies were their best guess but no one really took that possibility seriously, even though it wasn't too far from the truth. My daddy said it was demons, which would make sense because within a couple days of all the arrests, one of the killers claimed she was part of an anarcho-communist-feminist group called The Daughters of Lilith. One after the other, The Daughters of Lilith took responsibility for the murders. Rather than an outpouring of empathy coming from the public, there were waves and waves of protests all over the country. Protests against every value the superiors held sacred. Minorities against white privilege, women against patriarchy, trans against binary gender norms, poor against capitalism, and all the protestors joined forces against western civilization. Every norm we know went challenged. None of them were strong enough to withstand attack. Society was crumbling and soon the people would be dancing the Bacchus shuffle in the streets.

Scrolling through my thousands upon thousands of direct Instagram messages, I was reading love letters in between death threats and the one connective tissue between the two was everyone assumed that us Gaimans controlled the world. It gave me a lot of confidence and hope that the only boy I actually wanted might actually want me back. I typed his name into the search bar to stalk his profile, "Jesus Madrid."

Number Seven's profile had been inactive for as long as he was part of BDC. He only had a hundred followers to begin with, but still, every picture of him was undeniably hot. It seemed like he had traveled all around South and North America, meeting plenty of women along the way. I'd bite my lip, looking through his pictures and save the ones with him and a woman to remove the bitch and insert myself. We looked perfect together, Mexican pauper and white-half-Jewish princess. *Hot, hot, hot.*

I was so turned on by Jesus I masturbated for like ten minutes with a brown dildo I snuck into my room. Contraband like dildos can be acquired by ordering them with food and wine from the Chef or Somm. So, only the women of BDC can get contraband. I was just about to cum, pumping myself so fast, it was crazy. All sorts of sexual fantasies flooded my mind, gangbangs of men and women. Dicks of all races and sizes, fucking the shit out of me. Cum shooting in and on me.

"I'm your whore. All of you, take my virginity and do whatever the fuck you want with it."

Just as I felt ready to explode, I heard a knock at my door. I gasped and threw the wet, lubed up dildo across the room.

"Scarlet? It's me," Daddy said from behind the door.

"Come in," I shouted, panting.

Within the few seconds it took my daddy to open the door and walk over to the side of my bed, I was able to stabilize my breathing and re-zen myself.

"It's been an hour, dear."

"Hang on."

I took the phone and tried to close my Instagram so he wouldn't see Jesus' pictures, but he snatched it out of my hands before I could.

He saw the pictures I made, editing in myself next to Jesus like we were a couple. Staring at it, his cheeks turned a rose red and he smirked. His eyes floated up from the phone to me.

"Dear, you know Number Seven can't be distracted from his purpose. So, you better not be putting any of these feelings into action," he said, consolingly killing my dreams.

"I'm not...there just aren't any boys in here close to my age but him. What do you expect?"

"Now, honey, give Jesus some credit, he's a handsome man irrespective of his age."

"Daddy, you don't have anything to worry about, I was just playing around with pictures. I don't want Jesus...I'm just so lonely..." I started sobbing, delicately.

My daddy held me in his arms, rocking me back and forth.

"Baby, honey, dear, sweetheart...*it's okay.*"

"How is it okay? I'm young. I'm supposed to be out there, with all the other eighteen-year olds, living life. We live in New York City, the most fun city in the whole world and we're all cooped up here, miserable."

"You think it's fun down there? We're lucky to be cooped up here. Those people on the streets are sick, trust me...we made them that way."

"Am I sick for wanting to be with them?"

"Yes, but that's alright, because you're becoming healthier here, every day."

"Promise me I'll be princess of the world once this is all over."

"Baby, I've already promised you that a million times."

"I want to hear it again."

"Scarlet, when Bacchus finally fills the hearts of mankind and the world changes in our image, it'll be you, my Scarlet, who will be the most beautiful princess in the world. You won't just be as elegant, beautiful, and desired as a princess. You'll also be as powerful, revered, and inspiring as a queen."

I wrapped my arms around my daddy's neck then kissed him on the cheek.

"Thank you, Daddy...you're right, I'm happy I'm here."

"All better now?"

I nodded and he kissed me on the forehead.

"Alright baby, I'll see you soon."

"Bye, Daddy."

When Daddy reached the door, he turned back to look at me and softly said under his breath, "My queen."

The moment he closed the door behind him, I shot up out of my bed to retrieve the brown dildo so I could finish.

Part II
Winter's Wine

Chapter Seven
Workers of the World, Mobilize
Number Four – The Magician

"So rawly alive, I have become, that all Earthly feeling is experienced as spiritual pain, but I'm not complaining, because the Mad God has chosen me as his vessel and vessels shouldn't have feelings.
-Hersh, Number One, Vessel of the Mad God

Growing up in Brooklyn, my father was never home, leaving my sister, myself, and mother with no trace of him but the food he would put in our stomachs. Anthony De Palma, my dad, worked two jobs in construction, building the skyscrapers we take for granted today. Night and day. High and low. He'd build these shimmering behemoths from the ground up until the soot and dust, took its toll on his lungs, giving the man cancer. Never saw him smoke a cigarette in my life but who knows, I didn't see him much at all.

What was interesting about him, and I never knew this while he was alive, was that my father was a master Free Mason. As a Mason, his life's purpose was to rebuild the world in the image of Solomon's temple. To a Free Mason, divinity lies within the craft of building and every brick is a metric of the sacred. It puzzles me how a poor, dumb bastard like him, high in the organization and trusted with powerful secrets, didn't work a better job so he could spend more time with his family. Even still, the man had a profound impact on me. I don't think I've even touched the surface of what spiritual powers he passed down to me. Who knows what birthright is lying in wait in every strand of my DNA.

My father visiting me in the form of an angel was God's punishment upon me. Not the God of Bacchus Death Collective but the God of my childhood, the God of the church masses I would sleep through. Jesus Christ. I can only blame myself for all the lives my magick ritual has destroyed. All those women killing their children, then their husbands killing them...all those protests turned violent...that blood is on MY hands. I look at my face in the mirror and know I am no longer my father's son. I'm a monster.

Devoting my life to magick was a terrible mistake. "Do What Thou Wilt." That's what the creator of Thelema, his unholiness, Aleister Crowley teaches. Before ever studying Crowley, I had been living my life by this tenant. Brooklyn was a harsh place to call home in those days. You had to eat or be eaten. Kill or be killed. So, I ate and I killed. Did Aleister Crowley ever know how tough it was growing up poor on the streets? Fuck no, the only reason he had the privilege to develop his philosophy was because he came from a wealthy family. It's a rich-kid religion. So maybe my Father's judgement is what I needed to snap out of this brainwashing. I don't think I can do another ritual or cast another spell or summon anymore Gods. My heart's just not in it anymore. Guilt is the worst thing a magician can feel. Guilt will thwart any magical process. If your heart's not in it, the inter-dimensional gates will no longer bow and bend to your will. I must either learn to deal with this guilt, for killing thousands, or escape Bacchus Death Collective. Seeing as BDC needs me as a sacrifice, I don't see how they'll ever let me get out of the collective alive. The best I can do is convince them to let me out of the temple and escape. I just need the right plan and excuse. I also need the Banker to be a little drunk.

Chapter Eight
The Roman Dollar
Number Two – The Banker

"Pity serves the collective no function. A mad man feels no pity, ever. True strength comes from crushing those weaker than you. Only the weak will define strength in a way that validates their weakness. Sympathy, tenderness, guilt, and pity, all things that will distract the collective from its goal and eventually destroy it. If even one member of the collective ever feels for a second that they are sorry then that member must be killed."
-Hersh, Number One, Messiah of the Strong, Reaper of the Weak

Four little words to live by. Four little words to die for. Four little words, for little birds. "In God We Trust" inscribed on every dollar, quarter, nickel, dime and penny. So, what does the most powerful investment bank do to make people lose faith in God? Replace the dollar with a more Bacchic currency. *Introducing*, from the *sick* mind of Charles Gaiman...the Roman Dollar...THE BACCHIC DOLLAR. Every increment depicts the face of a different Roman God. The one true God of BDC, Bacchus, with his ivy crown, black beard and jovial smile, he adorns the hundred-dollar bill. Now, "In God We Trust" is replaced in the mind with *"With God, We Dance."* As for the actual bills though, any reference to God has been completely removed. Along with Bacchus, the gods Faunus, Venus, Jupiter, Mercury, and Apollo adorn the lesser bills. These sacred strips of paper have been tailored with threads infused with Cabernet Sauvignon. Thus, their green coloring takes on a delicious purple tint.

The advent of digital currencies changed how humans compete because now, any dollar can be mined and made out of thin air by any individual. Certain crypto-currencies can be generated simply by completing mathematical equations. Soon writing bad poetry will earn you digital dollars. So, what could possibly entice people to mine for Bacchic currency until it replaces the dollar? Easy, the more booze you drink, the more Bacchic currency you earn.

I don't think the public needs anymore help getting drunk, ever since the killings of their first borns, the lines for pubs have been stretching for blocks. It was only a matter of time now. When we all die as Hersh requires us, then all the mistakes made by Christianity will be corrected by the love of Lord Bacchus.

Lastly, you might assume, based on the names I've used previously, that I have a preference for the Roman names of these Gods over their original Greek names. You would be wrong in this case. Though there are many examples of choosing Bacchus over Dionysius, I should point out that my biggest plan is named after the Greek version. Usually, Americans name their lunar space expeditions after the queer God, Apollo, as in "Apollo 13," who appears on the two-dollar Bacchic bill. So, ironically, Bacchus Death Collective's mission to space, which is planned to occur fifteen years from now, presumably after I die, will be titled "Dionysius I."

Chapter Nine
Meditation Time
Number Six - The Chemist

"Money is the root of all evil but wine is beyond good and evil. Wine is the blood of life. The blood of Bacchus-Christ. Money can buy wine but now, thanks to Charles Gaiman, the only man I'd ever call father...now, drinking wine can make money."
-Hersh, Number One, God of Wine and Wealth

"Taste the sugar cube. The sugar cube tastes sweet...*but also strange*. You cannot pretend you're not tripping. This is the trip, there is no escape. You must suspend the cognitive mind and submit to mindlessness' spiral. The spiral is Hersh. Swirl and descend. Hear the droning of eternity within you. Swim in it. Observe the mind. Drown in the floods of abstraction. Chase the spiral. Together now, submerge and meet inside the collective stream of unconsciousness that links the Collective. Somewhere inside that ether, the abyss, is the gateway. Objects cannot exist in inner space but symbols can. The gateway is a symbol with which you can interact. It is the only thing visible in this invisible dimension. If you can find the gateway, enter and you will all join together, different sides of a spotless diamond. Raw and pure forever. If you cannot find the gateway then emerge out of the spiral. Swim back up for air. Open your eyes...slowly...do not punish yourself for your failure."

This is how I guide group meditation. All the men sit in a circle and close their eyes. First, I warm my old, brittle hands in the fire pit in the center of our meditation studio then I walk around placing cubes of sugar, reed honey, laced with various hallucinogenic euphoriants, particularly LSD, on their tongues. I instruct them to draw their tongues back into their mouths to let the sugar cubes dissolve and be swallowed. My guidance varies for every meditation based on my visions. The inter-dimensional gate between souls is a vision I've had ever since I traveled down the pupils of my casketed mother's corpse as a boy. I am sure it exists, this tunnel between people and dimensions, that the soul can travel freely through. You only need to find it once to gain access forever.

They call me the Chemist but I consider myself a harvester of the fruit of the gods. Even if those fruits are chemicals I've synthesized, I see them all as gifts from the creators. If I don't make it in the lab, I find it in the world and have it sent to the temple. The mad honey for instance, we import from Nepal. The honey itself draws its hallucinogenic properties from the rhododendron pollen that infuses it with Briana toxin.

The sugar cubes I've placed on everyone's tongues have been swallowed. Everyone's tripping in a circle. People are seeing and tasting and hearing colors that bleed up from the underlying layer beneath visible reality. The reducing valve has been loosened and everyone is experiencing the totality of information that surrounds them all the time. Even Hersh, the God-child, is overwhelmed, high off his holy ass. The total picture is revealed to men upon tripping, is always visible to a god, but this god, is melting under the sun that is illuminating his psychedelic experience. His clothes are slipping off, exposing his hybrid-genitals and his eyes are crisscrossed and rolled up in his head, then his mouth is frothing up a strange, bubbling green slime, crudely crusting over his lips. His chest and flailing arms convulse, but no one seems to be alarmed. This is Hersh's burden after all, he must let his body be taken by the Gods that they may drive him completely insane or kill him.

I close my eyes and meditate. I meditate by repeating my mantra. My mantra is a meaningless word made up of Vedic sounds. That meaningless word is *shiring*. Shiring, shiring, shiring, until I am diving deep into my inner space. In that blackness, the gateway appears. I swim through the gateway and link up to Hersh's mind. I can see his trip through his third-eye. He is suckling at the virgin's breast. She is lactating golden milk. She has turned into Apollo, the Roman God of truth, prophecy, healing, sun, light, and poetry.

I swim back through the gateway and sense there were three tunnels I could travel through to link up with the others. With three tunnels but four men present, one of the men must not have taken the sugar cube. I open my eyes and stare around the room. The Magician is crying hysterically, apologizing to everyone. The Banker is laughing madly but between cackles, he grinds his teeth and savagely bangs his fists on the ground. The Thief is simply sitting there, meditating in peace. He thinks he's clever, that one.

"If you protect your ego and never let it dissolve, it will consume you, you will never sense the God within. Keep your eyes closed and reduce life to one sublime particle.... Thief?"

The Thief opens his eyes.

"Chemist?" Slyly, the cynical bastard addressed me.

"Describe what you are feeling."

"I am an island meditating on itself. You are all waves crashing against my beaches, never submerging me underwater. I rose above you and there I shall always remain."

"Why did you not swallow the sugar cube?"

"I do not blindly follow anyone's orders. Not yours, not the Banker's, not Hersh's, no one's."

"Blasphemy. Hersh, did you hear that arrogant little prick?"

Hersh's eyes were rattling around in their sockets, he was completely lost to us at that moment.

"He can't hear you, Chemist. It's just you and I."

"If you don't have interest in participating in our rituals, why join Bacchus Death Collective at all?"

"I have my reasons, but curiosity mostly. You see, as a poet, I must temper my imagination by experiencing everything at least once. Even killing a man is something I desire doing. Taking your drugs though? Been there, done that. There's nothing left for you to teach me."

"You're so curious you're willing to risk being ritualistically murdered all to observe a cult? Your ego truly needs killing, Thief," I reached into my robe and rested my hand on the hilt of a knife I always kept on my person. "I hope you know if the others caught wind of your true feelings, you would be killed."

"Take your hands out of your robe. I know what you're holding onto in there. Rest assured, no one's quick enough to stab me."

I pulled the dagger out of my robe and showed it to the Thief. "I may be old but these drugs have given me the power to be at many places at once, I sit here but really, I'm all around you."

"What's taking you so long?"

The Thief stood up and smiled at me, mockingly. THE MOTHER FUCKER EVEN HAD THE AUDACITY TO WINK. *He thinks I'm not man enough. He thinks I don't mean my own words. That I don't have the balls.* The drugs may have dissolved my ego but damn it, *NO ONE DARES* smile and wink at me like that. Does he not realize he is speaking to a man of unparalleled GODLINESS? *Second only to Hersh, of course.*

I stood up and wielded my knife like a butcher. Slowly, I crept forward and with each step, the Thief giggled.

"Have you been smoking dope, too, slowpoke?" he said, clearly, he had no respect for my role in the collective.

I shouted a war cry and ran toward him, my blade glimmering over my head, ready to plunge into his face. When I finally reached the young man, he jumped in the air, did a spinning kick that hit me in the chest and sent me flying backward into the fire pit that was sitting in the center of our circle. It burned me for a terrible instant and I dropped the knife. The Thief stalked me like a silent panther and grabbed my face with his two hands and stuck my whole head back into the flames until roasting me alive. First, my hair burned to a crisp, then the skin of my scalp bubbled up and started baking. The dancing blades of fire stabbed through my head burning my brain and melting my eyeballs into putty. The last thing I saw was the Thief picking up and pocketing my knife. *The One who must die by fire had been sacrificed, all praise be to Bacchus.*

Chapter Ten
The Thief is the Killer
Number Seven – The Thief

"Gods do not inhabit the bodies of weak men. A strong man or in my case, a strong child, never asks to be a god, he is simply attuned because he has surpassed the boundaries of flesh. Man's brain is too small and body too fragile for souls like mine. Someday soon, I will leave this body and move onto another, like a hermit crab shedding its shell."
-Hersh, Number One, Strong Child, Godly Soul

I stood above the first man I ever killed without any sympathy in my heart. The Chemist wished for nothing more in death than I might consider myself guilty of deicide. Unlikely. Killing him had been like stepping on a worm. How his life escaped him under my force...it was thrilling. I looked around the room at my fellow Bacchae and could tell his screams did nothing to sober up the boys. When they'll return to reality, there will be no way of avoiding that awkward moment of being linked to the murder. I figured my best option was to stay put and catch up on some sleep. I walked over to the furthest corner from the drama and laid down, shut my eyes, and forgot about my evil deeds.

~ * ~

My eyes fluttered open with the Magician and Banker standing over me.

"Wake up," the Banker spoke harshly.

"What happened?" I asked and looked up at the Banker's red, trembling chin.

"You killed the Chemist."

"Did I?" I asked.

The Banker started slapping me as hard as he could till I scampered up to my feet.

"What are you, some kind of loon? You beat and burned him to death with your bare hands," he shouted at me, viciously.

"Oh my, that doesn't sound like something I would do...you sure?" I asked, making myself laugh inside.

"Yes."

"Hmph... Sorry," I shrugged.

The Banker was furious while the Magician's expression could not be gauged by anything but the dampness below his eyes.

"Why'd you do it, Number Seven?"

I gave myself a few healthy, memory recalling slaps to the back of the head. I was a regular Charlie Chaplin but a bit more sociopathic, in my own eyes.

"Oh wait, it's coming back to me now."

"A thief and a liar, should've known the two went hand and hand," the Banker groaned.

"Yes, I have it now...I killed the Chemist for committing blasphemy. He dared compare himself to Hersh, claiming that he was God."

"The Chemist's philosophy is that we *ALL* have the potential to be gods and acquire godliness, not that he *IS* God."

"With all due respect...you must not have been listening, Number Two. You couldn't hear the Chemist preaching over your crazed cackling."

"How dare you talk to me that way?"

"What difference does it make, anyway? Number Six became the one who must die by fire. We are one step closer to the beginning of the Bacchic Age," I reasoned.

"If you killed him, you must be punished. Number Six was indispensable to the cause...not to mention, he had rank over you. I will see to it your punishment will fit the crime. Perhaps I was wrong inviting a thief into our family in the first place."

"Why don't we ask Hersh? In fact, I refuse to be a victim of your witch hunt, Number Two. Hersh will decide whether I be punished or not."

"You can't ask him right now," the Magician finally spoke.

"Why not?"

I pushed the Magician and Banker out of the way and walked over to Hersh, who had been completely drained of life by the drugs and was trembling, half-dead on the floor. A pool of blood was leaking out from his halfling genitals and from out of the hole, a vine with a single black grape was growing.

"What am I looking at? Is this magic?"

The Magician walked over to my side.

"Yes, all fallout from the last ritual."

"Is he dead?" I asked.

"No, but he will die if this continues," the Magician sulked, hanging his head. "It's all my fault. I should've known he couldn't handle another possession."

"This place manifests the murderer in us all, we should be more compassionate to one another and not try to punish each other for our natural responses to this environment."

Suddenly, Hersh's pupils drifted back down to the center of his eyes and he seemed to stare up at us, blinking rapidly.

"Number Seven, Four...help me up."

The Magician and I carefully pulled Hersh off the floor.

"Someone needs to remove this thing sticking out of me."

The Banker walked over and casually, without warning, plucked the vine out of Hersh, causing the child excruciating pain. Hersh then fell right back to his knees, bleeding.

"Show some remorse, Number Two," the Magician fumed.

"I plan to keep this, Magician," said the Banker as he stuck the vine in his pocket. "You might have a spell you could use it for but I don't care, something this special either needs to end up in my collection...or stomach."

"You're disgusting," the Magician replied.

"What about Number Seven? Let's not lose focus. Hersh, it appears that the Thief has killed the Chemist by fire."

"I'm in no state to pass judgement right now."

The Banker laughed, heartily, "Nonsense...you're a God."

Terribly weakened, Hersh stiffly turned his head toward me, staring into my eyes. With one look, I silently communicated this to him, "I'm sorry, my dear boy, you do not deserve all the pain the world has dealt you."

"Why did you kill the Chemist, Thief?" Hersh asked.

"He claimed to be your superior, Lord Bacchus. He claimed to be God and blasphemers must die."

"I agree," Hersh nodded, wagging his poor head up and down. No amount of trauma could kill the murderer in him.

"I don't believe him, Lord Bacchus," the Banker contested.

"I do and that's all that matters. The Thief will go unpunished and you will not mention this again, Number Two."

I looked up at the Banker and smiled from ear to ear. It looked like steam could rise up out of his red, burning face at any second.

"What's the matter?"

"How am I supposed to get the drugs I need to consume every day?"

"Easy, we live in New York City. I can get them for you tonight."

"Really? Thanks for volunteering... Number Four, you'll go with him to make sure he stays out of trouble."

I could see the Magician's face light up.

"As you wish, sir," the Magician said, hiding his excitement.

"Take our Lord to his bed then you will await further instruction before leaving."

"Yes, sir," the Magician said.

"Dress warm. It's fucking freezing out there."

The Banker then looked to me. As important as it was to show my obedience at this moment, all I could muster up was a wink.

"Such a rebellious young man, I can tell it's almost killed you many times."

"Yes, but for all those times, choosing obedience in those moments would've surely done me in."

The Magician and I picked Hersh up and carried him out of the meditation studio and into his quarters. Hersh's room was a Bacchic palace with beautiful fountains that shot wine out of golden statues of dolphins, bulls, and lions. His bed was a small twin size covered in gold satin bedding and surrounded with a golden frame. On his bed were sprawled the dolls and action figures he used to play with long before anyone ever called him a God. I took Hersh's toys off the bed and the Magician gently set him down.

"Thank you, Number Four," Hersh softly grumbled and closed his eyes before falling fast asleep.

"No, thank you, my Lord," the Magician replied. Hearing this made a tear roll down Hersh's cheek.

I saw a small square photograph poking out from between Hersh's two pillows and without the Magician seeing, I pocketed it faster than the speed of light. I couldn't get a good look at the photo but as soon as I had a second alone, I'd take a peek.

"Come on, let's go," the Magician waved me out the room with him.

I followed him through the royal doors and we went back to our rooms to layer up on the warmest clothes we had.

Chapter Eleven
Born Into The Water
Number Eight – The Virgin

"What happens when a god dies? Does the world shift on its axis? Do the poles melt? Do the seas overflow? Do people miss you? Do they even remember? They remember Christ, but it's only been two thousand years. Far more powerful gods are now long forgotten. Perhaps if I preached peace and piety, I would leave a longer legacy. I'm in so much pain and feel so upset that the idea of saying love is greater than all, might actually do the trick and kill me."
-Hersh, Number One, the Dying God

I dream of the day that wealth is repugnant to women. That their reaction to gold and diamonds is to vomit. That they sooner fuck plumbers than bankers. If only the Thief could see inside my heart and touch my naked body. He'd know my love for him was genuine and unaffected by my privilege. Not a night goes by that I don't touch myself thinking of his smooth, brown skin and long, raven-black hair. I am a virgin with a harlot's heart and a whore's intuition. A whore can take one look at a man and know the worst porn he jacks off to...and in some cases, still consider fucking them.

That's why I look at my father with such repulsion. Because he looks at the world through eyes that have watched every sort of bestial, incestuous, pedophilic rape fantasy. He'll always be a creepy old pervert no matter how much power and money he acquires.

I was scrolling through my Instagram feed until arriving on my father's profile. There were pictures of him at elegant dinners, ballroom dances, and fashion galas with beautiful women every night. Even times he was alone, in his room, drinking, there would be pictures posted of him somewhere else.

Just then, my father walked into my room and quickly, I hid his phone under my ass and sat on it, hoping he didn't see anything.

"Scarlet."

"What, Dad?"

"Number Six is DEAD."

"Who?"

"Number Six. The Chemist."

"Oh."

"He had a daughter, a few years older than you, and I wanted to call her and tell her but when I went into my room and looked for my phone, it was missing from my cabinet."

"That's odd."

"Don't patronize me, Scarlet. I know you. Now give me my phone."

"You think *I* took it?"

"Yes. Now give it to me before I have to punish you. I'm very fucking angry right now, Scarlet."

"I don't have it."

"Stop lying to me."

He slapped me across the face so hard he broke my nose and sent me off my bed, onto the floor. The phone now rested in plain sight where my ass had been. My father just shook his head and took it.

"Why did you disobey me?"

Wheezing and gasping for air and crying so hard I thought I could die, I tried to make a plea for mercy, "I'm sorry. Please, Daddy. Don't hurt me."

His breath nearly caved in his chest and his veins were pulsating at the sides of his head and neck. I had never seen him so furious.

"I have to hit you again, Scarlet...I can't not hit you again." His lip and fists were trembling with rage.

He walked over to me and with one hand, lifted me off the ground by my hair. Pulling my head back, he saw the blood running out of my nostrils and down my mouth to my chest.

"How many times do I have to tell you, you're not allowed to use my phone without permission?"

"Never again. I'll never ask for the phone again," I croaked.

"I don't believe you," Daddy shouted as he punched me in the stomach. It sounded like a shotgun went off inside me.

"Cunt. Stupid little fucking cunt."

I couldn't even beg for my life at this point. To beg I'd have to be able to breath and my lungs felt like a crumpled-up accordion. Gasping for air, my only compulsions were to cry and spit up blood.

"Should I hit you again?"

I vomited on his shoes.

"Yes? No?"

"No," I squeaked, in excruciating pain.

"Good...now you know to never go into my quarters again. You are my daughter...I own you...so you will do as I say, understand?"

"Yes," I whispered and passed out, face flat on the floor.

I woke up in my bed an hour later. All the lights were off and I could barely make out the shadowy shapes of my body. I could sense I was in new clothes. My broken nose was repaired and the blood was cleaned off my face. I was still in enormous pain but when I tried to stand up, I saw a shackle wrapped around my foot attached to a chain hanging down from the ceiling. I laid there and dreamed that somehow the Thief would rescue me. He would kiss me softly and carry me far away from here. We would start a family and his touch would never cause me pain...unless I was asking for it.

Chapter Twelve
Apollo Sleeps
Number Seven – The Thief

"Nothing pains me more than the memories of the abuse I suffered and nothing makes me more furious than seeing an adult abuse another child. Growing up how I did, with a body like mine, I was beaten for all the sins my parents committed to get punished with a curse like me being born. I cry every night remembering it. Gods cry too. Hades cried tears of lead. Bacchus cries tears of tannic wine."
-Hersh, Number One, the Crying God, the Abused Bacchus

The Magician and I could hear the Virgin's screams all the way from the door of the Banker's room. It sent chills up our spines. We both trembled in wait for the Banker to come out of his daughter's room and give us our instructions on leaving the temple.

"The man has to be stopped," the Magician whispered, shaking his head.

"He's here to die, it's only a matter of time, and a short time at that."

"Then what? He inspires the world to be more like him? The girl is here to die too. You think she volunteered for that fate?"

"We did, didn't we?"

The Magician bowed his head, "You're right. We've done something irredeemable."

"Why do you think we chose this?"

"Magical possession is the only answer that makes sense to me...how else can good men commit such evil but by some mad man's spell?"

"Who's to say we are good though?"

"You don't consider yourself as such?"

"Honestly...no."

The Magician just shut his mouth. He had no interest in delving any

48

deeper into my logic. If I called myself evil, he would take my word for it, and he was right to do so.

The Banker softly closed the door to his daughter's quarters. His hands were covered in blood too pink to be his. That man could walk through walls, there was so much force behind him as he approached us. Our fear was palpable and with it, the Banker would control us like a pair of marionettes.

"Alright, you two pussies are going to get my drugs on the street like how I used to do things before there was a Bacchus Death Collective."

"Yes, sir," I said.

"I want an ounce of cocaine and twenty ecstasy pills. You're going to buy it from a nigger and once you make the deal, you're going to kill him."

Warily, the Magician's eyes floated over to the side to look at me.

"What's the matter, Number four? Having second thoughts?" The Banker got in his face.

"No. I want to do this, sir."

"Good. I invited you so you could supervise the Thief. I don't trust him like I do you, Magician."

"I will regain your trust, sir," I said.

"No, you won't but the Magician might. If either of you feel so bold as to run, then mark my words, you'll be dead by morning."

"We'll return in a few hours," I assured the Banker.

"Go before the bars close, that's where you'll find drugs," the Banker said, as he pulled out a roll of bills and tossed them at me. I caught and stuffed them into the same pocket I had been keeping Hersh's photograph.

"See you later, Number Two," I bowed.

"Goodbye," the Magician repeated.

The Magician and I walked through the great portal doors of the temple and for the first time since I entered, I made my way out of this place. We were in total disbelief that the Banker could be so stupid as to allow us this chance.

The doors led to a black marble hallway at the end of which was a Latino security guard sitting behind a desk in front of an elegant glass elevator. This was the first time the guard had seen anyone exit the temple, and his eyes opened up like large opals, glossy with fear.

"Hey...llo, how...how can I, um...help you?" the guard stammered.

"We need to go down to the ground level," I stated.

"No problem."

The guard jumped out of his chair and swiped a keycard through the elevator's digital lock. He then pressed the single button on the outside of the elevator and together we waited for the capsule to arrive. I could tell the guard had hundreds of questions he wanted to ask us just swimming around in his head, but he was too timid to even make a peep.

"Do you work here every day?" I asked.

"Every night," the guard answered.

"Have you ever wondered what goes on in there?"

"All the time. We hear...*rumors*, all the workers in this building. Is it true? Do you have orgies all day and night?"

"If I told you, I'd have to kill you," I joked.

The guard didn't seem too amused by the cliché and went pale, turning away from me.

"Don't listen to my brother, you have nothing to worry about," the Magician comforted him.

The guard smirked and nodded. We had retarded the poor fellow.

"There will come a day that I will need your help, sir," the Magician began, gaining the guard's total attention. "You will serve a very important purpose. One that will help all of humanity."

"Really? I always thought I might," the guard professed, teary eyed.

"Yes, just keep your eyes and ears open and remember my face. I will tell you to disobey your orders and you will listen," the Magician told him.

The guard was in total awe until the elevator arrived and then, trembling and unsteady on his feet, he shuffled inside the glass capsule and swiped his keycard into another digital lock inside. He then pressed the button reading "G" and left the Magician and I in the elevator, so he may return to his post. We waved goodbye as the capsule doors closed and gently glided down to the bottom of Gaiman's massive skyscraper. The lights of Manhattan took on a diffused glow through the chilly fog and snow.

The elevator stopped at the lobby, where all the suited squares stared at us with unyielding curiosity. We strut out of the building until the marble beneath our feet transitioned into glorious concrete.

We were hoping our memories of the New York we knew prior to BDC would come flooding back to us, but the first thing we noticed upon exiting the Gaiman Building was winter's bitter cold. We were freezing through our four layers of clothing.

In what could be our last opportunity to ever adventure through this or any city, the obvious choice was to disobey our orders and see what trouble we could get into. There were women and booze and kind strangers and music waiting for us around every corner. The Magician and I began walking together down 62nd street but after a few minutes, as the city's noise bellowed louder and drew closer, he turned to me and started walking backwards, seemingly elated.

"I'm going to run and there's nothing you can do to stop me."

"*What? Where would you go?*"

"Home."

"Our home is the temple."

"No, it's not. I'm never going back there again."

"I beg you to reconsider, it'll be my neck too."

The Magician spun around on his heel as fast as he could and sprinted up the street, exerting every last electron of drive in him. I ran after him but didn't have as much desire to catch him as he had to escape. It was too cold to sprint, trying to catch my breath felt like huffing in needles that scraped the inner lining of my lungs.

What is a poor Thief with thousands of dollars of someone else's money supposed to do alone in Manhattan? I figured I'd just follow the noise. The first place I wound up was on Broadway Avenue. Death in every frosty breath, the streets were filled with vibrant life. I could recognize Bacchus in them almost immediately, the seed had been planted long before BDC. Deep down, these people all wanted civilization to collapse. I saw street performers getting sick with cold, Blacks howling happily on their way to the white-free, colored clubs and bars, Whites either frozen timid or turned into party tyrants, and Latinos laughing and teasing at every passerby. Everyone, of every race and class, had a bottle, can, or flask in hand and were taking sharp swigs of booze. Drunken eyes half open, half closed, the holy night hiccups heavy. Among the living, were the dead, frozen stiff and we would just walk past them, not letting sympathy slow us down. The first bar I entered was Broadway Dive, it had been so long since I dove so deep.

The floor was sticky and the smell was grotesque, for too long my nostrils had been treated to the pleasant fragrances of rich living but now, among the cockroach people, they were invaded by the foul odors of piss, vomit, and sweaty, unwashed bodies. The warmth made it all tolerable, though. My veins needed tightening with a stiff shot, so I approached the bar and promptly ordered tequila. In a dirty shot glass, the barkeep topped me off with a cheap, Spanish bottle. I slammed the shot and reached into my pocket to pay the man but pulling out what felt like a bill, I accidently retrieved the photo I had stolen from Hersh. I took a good look at it, hunching over so no one else could sneak a peek.

There he was, just a baby, blonde curls and blue eyes, and lips hanging open with plenty of adorable *goo-goo*. His parents looked mild-mannered, blue-collar, and devoutly Christian. They stood in front of a blue house, with beautiful Cypress trees hanging into the frame. They were blonde and blue eyed like their baby and there was no foreshadowing of Bacchic inspiration to come. It was a pure moment in a modest, white, American life.

"Ey man, you can't pay for that shit with a fuckin' picture."

I snapped back to reality and looked up at the barkeep who was looming over me, bothered that I was anchoring him down.

"Sorry."

I shoved the picture back into my pocket and pulled out the roll of dollars the Banker gave me. Looking at the dollars, I noticed these were not American bills. Each had a picture of Bacchus, drinking from a bottle of wine in the center. I pulled out a bill and showed it to the barkeep.

"You accept these?"

"Course."

The barkeep took the bill and moments later, returned with various bills featuring different Gods and Goddesses. Just then, a beautiful Puerto Rican sat next to me and drew my attention to her face. She wore so much make-up, she looked like a cartoon, a mix between Selena and Jessica Rabbit but wearing dark blue and with nails painted midnight.

"The Goddess of love is all you'll need, Mijo. For her, I'd give you the greatest night of your life," she said, as she plucked a Venus from my stack of bills.

"I'm looking for cocaine but sex would be a nice bonus, know where I can find any?"

She graced her cool hand across my warm cheek, caressing it and erecting the hairs on the back of my neck.

"You're going to need more Gods than that, babe."

I pulled out the roll of Bacchuses and saw her eyes grew wide.

"Come with me, Mijo. We'll go back to my place and call a friend of mine."

"Sounds good. What's your name?"

"Call me Selena Rabbit."

"I'm Jesus Madrid."

We kissed and I slid off my stool to follow her out of the bar and back into the snowfall. Quickly, she hailed a cab and we both got in.

"50th and 67th," she told the driver and off we went.

Selena pulled out her phone and started typing away.

"I just texted my homie, how much do you want?"

"An ounce...ask if he has any ecstasy."

"I'm sure he does."

"I'll need ten pills."

"Okay, I'll let him know."

The cabbie drove us out of Manhattan into Queens and as the neighborhood's skin darkened, the buildings decayed. We arrived at Selena's apartment and she walked me up a few flights of old creaking stairs to her door. She pointed to my shoes.

"This is an Asian household."

I took off my soggy boots and placed them onto her shoe rack. Her apartment was full of paintings in amber hues and musty furniture.

"Make yourself comfortable," she told me, lovingly.

I plopped down on her couch and sprawled my limbs out to achieve maximum comfort.

"You hungry?" she asked.

"Starving...got any rabbit?"

She laughed, "No, just pastelon."

"What that?"

"Green Roast Beef."

"Heat some up."

She smiled and put all her yellow teeth on display between her blue lips. The pan of green beef was chilling in her fridge until she threw it in the oven. Selena tango'd all by herself out of the kitchen and back to me. She kneeled between my legs, resting her midnight fingers on both of my knees.

"My friend will be here in thirty minutes, the pastelon will be hot in ten."

"If you have an idea how we could spend that time, then don't ask for my permission, just do it."

She unzipped my pants and pulled out my cock. It had been so long since a truly beautiful woman touched it. I closed my eyes and imagined it was the Virgin's mouth my dick was swimming in. Her beady brown eyes were fixed upon my face, to call those eyes loving was an understatement, they were obsessed. After ten long minutes, I finished in her mouth and wilted like a blown-out dandelion.

The smell of the pastelon awakened my blood thirst. Selena wiped her lips and walked over to the kitchen to take it out of the oven. She made me a plate of the green beef over rice and I scarfed down every last morsel, grain, and drop. After I finished, I leaned back into the couch and rubbed my stuffed stomach.

A knock came at the door and Selena scampered over to let the dealer in. He was black, just what the Banker ordered. The dealer sat down beside me and showed me what he thought was the peace sign but was actually the hand sign for war, two separated, distant fingers.

"Watts."

"Jesus."

"How much yayo you want?"

"Ounce of cocaine, ten ecstasy pills."

"I got you."

"You got a scale?"

"I don't take that shit with me, partner."

"Don't worry about it. How much do I need to *payo*?"

"I got you for a band and a half," Watts stated, rolling his eyes.

I took fifteen Bacchus bills out of the roll and handed them to Watts. He looked at them then jerked his neck back at Selena.

"Selena. *Bitch*...you didn't say nothing about him having this funny money, bull shit."

"Why does it matter? It's not fake."

"They don't accept them fucking bearded dollars everywhere."

"Not yet," I answered. "Here."

I threw in an extra five bills and he took them reluctantly.

"You're lucky Selena is my homegirl. Pleasure doin' fuckin' business," Watts reached into his jacket and slammed down a dense bag of cocaine on the table. Then out of his pants pocket, he pulled out the ten pills.

I snagged the pills then leaned back into the couch.

"Would either of you like a line?"

"Sure," Watts nodded.

"*Mhmmm,*" Selena purred.

I opened the bag of cocaine and scooped a small mound of powder on the side of the Chemist's knife. I laid the coke down on a piece of paper then pulled out Hersh' photograph to lay it over the powder, so I could crush it into a fine dust with the hilt of the knife. Once crushed, I made four lines, two for Watts, two for Selena. They fiendishly snorted both rails, leaning their heads back to let the cocaine slush down their throats.

I sealed the bag up and shoved it in my pocket.

"What's wrong? You too good to get high with us?" Watts asked.

I stood up off the couch and walked out of the apartment without saying goodbye, puzzling them both.

~ * ~

Royal screams soared into the night over Queens. Frost and bloodshed, I reached into my pocket, pulled out a pill, and popped it into my mouth. In about an hour, I'd be feeling like I won the fucking lottery. I kept my hands in my pockets to keep them warm but also grip the Chemist's knife with vicious intent. Making love on MDMA is sensational but committing violence on it is pure electricity. Even thinking about it put a slickness in my step.

The layer of ice between my feet and the concrete couldn't muffle the heavy bass that was vibrating the block from the Amadeus Night Club. The line was long and snaking all the way down to the corner. I approached the bouncer and pulled out three Bacchuses and stuffed them into his coat pocket. Without question or gratitude, he unhooked the velvet rope for me and I walked right in, much to the dismay of the dying, waiting in line.

The rap music was intense and bounced between Spanish and English lyrics. Blacks and browns packed the Amadeus, warming each other up. They would bombard the bar for drinks and once they polished them off, they would take an object, a sort of purple breathalyzer, and blow into it. Their breath would indicate how drunk they were with a dollar amount.

"What is that thing?" I asked one clubber blowing into a breathalyzer.

"What thing?" he asked once finished blowing.

"The thing you blew into."

"What? Have you been living under a fuckin' rock? It measures how drunk you are and rewards you with cash accordingly but only 'em Bacchus bills."

"I see. Where do I get one?"

"Any liquor store."

"I'll look into it, thanks."

"No problem, bro."

The ecstasy was starting to hit me, I was sweating, burning in side. The lights would hum, streak, and dazzle as I rubbed up against everybody around me. Male and female arms around my body, hard pounding hip-hop, my heart beats ballistically. I was on top of the bottom, Bacchus bills were shooting up from my pockets and raining down on everyone, sticking to their naked, sweaty flesh. My soul stirred with high-fashion frenzy, love was in the air, and I am the air, water, fire, and Earth. The clock struck two am and a thought had struck my brain, busting my buzz. I couldn't return to the temple without the Magician. If I did, the punishment would be death and the BDC would fail. I snuck out of the dancing mass back into the fray of snow outside. A cab was lying in wait, I told the cabbie to take me to the only place that the Magician ever told me he visited.

"Brooklyn."

"Where in Brooklyn?"

"A good bar. Not fancy. Blue collar."

"You coming to the meeting tonight?"

"Meeting?"

"At the Longbow."

"Take me there, I guess I'll meet."

The cabbie drove off and flew onto Grand Central Parkway. The city lights bled into liquid pools in my owl pupils. After a slew of sharp turns, the crazed cabbie arrived in front of the Longbow, where multiple cops waited at the door. I stepped out of the cab and as did the cabbie.

"You coming in too?" I asked.

"Of course, brother...we're in this together," the cabbie crossed over to my side of his cab and put his arm around me to lead me into the Longbow. When we walked up to the entrance, one of the cops stopped me, placing his palm in the center of my chest.

"You in the right place, pal?"

"He's here for the meeting," the cabbie told the cop.

"You want to make a change in the world, brother?" the cop asked me.

"Yes. *For the children*," I answered, sounding sincere.

"Come inside and share the hearth."

"Thank you, brother," I replied.

The cabbie and I entered the Longbow to find it filled with blue collars standing before a stage where a surly speaker in a mechanic's jumpsuit, addressed the people on a microphone.

"My child was killed by my own wife. We were married for ten years. Our son was eight. He was our miracle. I wasn't even home to try and stop her. I was at work. My younger son, Hector, saw it happen and had to stay with *that* BITCH until I came home and walked into the kitchen and saw my baby boy, my Carlos, on the table cut down his middle and without his head. I wrestled Hector away from my wife and was able lock us in the bathroom away from her. I called the police, completely torn to pieces. Thank God Hector was alright. I don't know what the reason for all this craziness is but I feel in my gut that it's all somehow connected. The murders, the protests, class war, race war, the fucking alcoholism run rampant...someone's controlling us like a bunch of pawns in chess. Don't think for one second, that you and your family is safe at home from these people. *I don't care how many guns you got*. They're controlling you through the TV, through your fucking phone, in the goods you consume, in the things you eat and drink...here..." The mechanic reached into his pocket and pulled out his wallet. He unfolded his wallet to retrieve a Bacchus bill to show the crowd. "Look what they're shoving down our throats now. They're killing our faith and culture."

The audience agreed with every word out of the mechanic's mouth. "Last thing I got to say before I go, these rich folk, they see this moment in history as the end of some failed experiment and we're they're experiment. If we value our lives and our children, then we can't take this sitting down. We can't vote or protest this away. We have to fight till the bloody end," the mechanic finished with a raised fist in the air.

The crowd erupted into cheer, raising their fists with the mechanic as he stepped off the stage. A heroic looking character in a fireman's uniform stepped onstage and took the mechanic's place at the microphone.

"I see some new faces in the audience. If any of you would like to come up here and tell us your story, please do. Don't be shy, we're all brothers here. It's no good being timid in a war, so if you're new, introduce yourself," the fireman finished and a wave of awkward stares befell me, urging me to step forward.

I looked around, staring at all the hard faces staring back at me. These were not the beautiful people. The forgotten middle and lower classes had gathered under the banner of hatred for the shadow forces that controlled them. I decided to just turn around and cut my losses. I didn't have a story to tell them tonight. I was about to make my way out the bar when another man slithered through the packed crowd and got up onstage.

A voice came from behind me, "My name is Salerno De Palma..."

My head spun with shock and glee, it was just the man I was hoping to see. Number Four, the Magician, took the stage.

"I don't have a real job like most of you guys in here. I'm a magician," he addressed the crowd.

"You gonna pull a rabbit out of your ass for us?" one audience member joked, causing an uproar of laughter.

The Magician smirked slyly, "No, but I can help you fight this war." The crowd applauded and whistled for the Magician.

"How are you gonna do that?" the fireman asked.

"The first rule of a war is to know your enemy. All you guys see is the pain they cause you but I see the perpetrators. I see them every day. I see their faces, their kids, I see them drunk and high when they decide to fuck you all over."

"This better not turn into some racist or anti-Semitic shit, pal, or else we're gonna kick your ass the fuck out of our bar," one patron shouted.

"No...these people that hurt you are called the Bacchus Death Collective."

"*The what?*" the crowd asked.

"Bacchus, the Roman God whose face is on that blood money. Death as in the end of life. Collective, a group of chosen people. Bacchus Death Collective wants to drive you insane."

"If you see them every day, how come you don't do nothing about it?"

"Because I used to be one of them. It kills me to admit it, I cast the spell that made your wives murder your sons."

"Oh shit," I said under my breath, sure that the crowd was about to rip him to pieces.

Immediately, everyone erupted into a blind rage, throwing their drinks at the Magician and taking the stage to grab and dismantle him. They were pulling him in every direction, punching his face, biting him, scratching him, trying to break his bones in half. Pocket knives jabbing his flesh, he didn't let a single blow keep the microphone away from his mouth.

"If you kill me, you'll never stop them. If you kill me, you'll never find them. I'm the only one that can help you. Either let me live or it's your lives. I came here to help you. I came to save you. I came here to kill them with you," the Magician desperately shouted.

I couldn't just let the Magician get killed with my ass on the line too. I jumped over people, stomping on their heads and shoulders to get on stage. When I reached the Magician, I grabbed the microphone out of his hand and shouted into it. "Let him go. Don't hurt him. I SAID LET HIM GO, GOD DAMN YOU."

To my surprise, all the men heeded my plea and stopped ravaging him. The stage cleared of everyone, leaving the Magician lying on the floor, battered and bleeding and struggling to breathe.

"Why the hell should we listen to you?"

"Was your son murdered?"

"Don't tell us what to do, this fucker ruined our lives."

The crowd berated me with shouting during until I brought the microphone back to my mouth.

"Listen to us, we're the guys that will be responsible for good defeating this evil."

"Oh really? A pussy like you?"

I thought for a second, steadied my breath, closed my eyes, and spoke into the microphone. "Good always defeats evil."

"How the fuck do you know?"

"Because if evil ever defeated good then this world would've been destroyed long ago."

The room went quiet until the Magician pulled himself back up to his feet and took the microphone from me.

"Who among you is your leader?" the Magician asked.

The fireman stepped forward, "Me. My name is Chris Bordin."

"Chris, if you trust me, I can help you stop this insanity."

The Magician stuck his bleeding hand out to Chris for him to shake. Chris stared at the hand and fearlessly shook it and made peace.

"Forgive us, Salerno...if you come with me to the kitchen, we can clean you up and figure out how you can help us."

"Thank you. Please."

"Make way, brothers," Chris commanded.

The crowd parted like the Red Sea and Chris helped the Magician walk between the two masses of men to the back of the pub and into kitchen. Once the Magician disappeared behind the door, the crowd's eyes moved from him, back to me.

"So, who are you, man? Are you friends with that guy?"

"I have no friends. I'm a loner in search of the night's best party..."

"Last call," the bartender shouted from the back of the pub.

"Looks like that party's over now, though...I'm going to go smoke a cigarette."

I stepped down from the stage and passed through the people to the exit without being harmed or bothered. Outside, I found a group of cops smoking Marlboros.

"Can I bum one?"

"Sure, brother."

The cop gave me a cigarette and lit it for me. I smoked it and watched the smoke spiral-dance in mathematical irreverence. I felt like the Diogenes of NYC, a philosopher and a funny bastard. I stared at the cop and realized he was no ordinary badge. I recognized him by his fuzzy, grey moustache and the tiny scar on his chin. This was police chief Merle Swanson that bummed me a cigarette, head-honcho of the NYPD. Wanting to fuck with him, I conceived of a quick test of character I could put him through. Right then and there, I took out the bag of cocaine, scooped out a bump and snorted it.

"Whoa, do that shit around the corner if you have to, brother," Swanson advised me.

What a failure, just like I expected him to be. *Pathetic*. No collective or mob or party is free from hypocrisy and corruption. Sorry, folks. Heroes, like messiahs and gods, don't exist. There are no right answers, only wrong people.

"How do you do it?"

I turned around and exhaled smoke into the Magician's face as he limped out of the pub.

"Do what?"

"Always end up in the right places?" he replied, wafting away the smoke from his face.

"I give people the impression I always have the right to pass unchallenged. You do that all the time and life will lead you directly to its power source. That's how I ended up in BDC."

"Makes sense. You ready to go home?"

"I'm happy you had a change of heart."

"Yeah, well, you had my back in there. If it wasn't for you, I might not be here right now."

"That's right, so you might say...you owe me one."

"Maybe I do, so long as it's reasonable."

"Would you kill for me?"

"No, I'm through with that."

"Would you steal for me?"

"No."

"I'll figure something out eventually, let's go."

We walked until we reached the 77th street subway station. I helped the Magician the whole way underground. There was a hot reek of rot that consumed the station when the R train came barreling through the tunnel and halted at our feet. We sat across a homeless man, humping the seats he laid face down upon, half conscious. The R took us to 36th street, where we had to transfer off the R to the D. We got on the D and it took us to Columbus Circle. Once the train took us as close to home as possible, I helped the Magician back to the city's surface to keep on walking.

On the walk back home, we passed a bookstore. It had been so long since I had even held a good book in my hands that I had to stop. Beacon Books was closed at this hour but seeing as I'd have no other chance to leave the temple, I had to take this opportunity to take what I would otherwise purchase.

"What are you doing? We have to keep going," the Magician barked at me.

"Hang on, I want some books," I replied looking for a heavy object.

"Oh no, please don't...we're so close to home," the Magician begged me.

Stealing books is lowly but throwing bricks through bookstore windows is just vile. Every inch of that window shattered in a rain of glass when that brick came crashing through it. I strode right into the store as the alarms rang and buzzed at ear-splitting volumes all around me. It would only be moments until the police arrived but thankfully, I knew how to navigate through any bookstore to find exactly what I need. I got all the basic books to educate someone on how to think subversively. I snagged the books of Darwin, Freud, Payne, Dostoevsky, Jung, and Plato and carried them in my coat out of the bookstore.

I met the Magician outside and we slyly strolled away from the noisy scene until a cop car pulled up to the store, stopped, and shined it's high-beams on us.

"You two. Stop right there. Hands in the air," the police commanded over their loud speaker.

We both raised our hands over our heads.

"Fucking idiot," the Magician sneered at me.

The cops rolled up to our side and got out of their car with their guns drawn, pointed at us.

"Get down on the ground."

The Magician showed no fear and with his arms still raised over his head he spoke, "Brothers, we are members of the resistance on special mission from Chris Borden and Chief Merle Swanson."

The cops lowered their weapons until the Magician took one hand and balled it into a fist. He then took that fist and laid it flat against his heart. "The forces of darkness will never prevail and the Brotherhood of Righteous Men will never fail."

The cops withdrew their weapons and got back into their car.

"Forgive us, brothers, we will take care of this. Whatever reason you had for doing what you did, we are sure it was for a righteous cause. Peace and strength be with you, brothers."

"Thank you, brother," I added.

The cop glared at me then happily waved goodbye to the Magician. They drove back to the bookstore and began taping off the scene.

We kept walking until we reached the Gaiman Building. The two of us could not deflect a single stare. The Magician was limping, with his clothes covered in blood and my pupils were as big as portals still coming down from the ecstasy. We approached the elevator and a guard nodded at us and swiped his keycard for it to open. We stepped inside the glass capsule and the guard swiped his keycard again and pressed the top button which read "Penthouse': The elevator took us back up to the temple and as it shot us up, the sun rose over the horizon and called an end to the night.

When the elevator reached the temple floor, we stepped out and walked past the guard at his desk.

"Good morning," said the guard as we did nothing to acknowledge him.

We arrived at the temple doors and saw there were no knobs or handles.

"How do we get back inside?" I asked the Magician.

The Magician planted a kiss on the door and it opened. We stepped inside and immediately, the Banker approached us.

"Looks like you two had one hell of a night," he sized us up and down, clearly fiending for a fix. "Where are my drugs?"

I pulled out his cocaine and pills and handed them to him.

"Did you kill whoever sold this to you?"

"Yes," I lied.

"Okay, give me back the money."

I pulled the roll of bills out and he clearly noticed it was much thinner than what he expected.

"*Hmph*...well, by the looks of you, the money was spent in praise of Bacchus, so I can't complain. I'll be in my chambers, don't disturb me."

The Banker scampered away, excitedly. Now, no longer attached at the hip, the Magician and I immediately went our separate ways. The Magician took off to his room but I didn't go back to mine, I had business elsewhere first, in a room that I was completely forbidden from ever entering. I wanted to trespass and infringe one last time before falling asleep.

I arrived at the Virgin's door and took a deep breath before quietly pushing it open. The first thing I heard were her whimpers. Sobbing, she appeared so weak and broken.

"Please...please, don't hurt me anymore...I'm in so much pain," she didn't realize it was me.

"Don't worry, princess...I would never dream of hurting you."

I walked over to her bed and sat down by her side. She opened her eyes, releasing two streams of tears, and looked up at me with a joy so true and sheer it felt like I saved a life from drowning.

"Oh...it's you," she said, hiding her excitement.

"Hello, princess."

"Are you here to rescue me?"

"Yes."

She smiled even though the gesture caused her broken nose pain.

"How?"

"Here."

I reached into my coat and took out the books I stole earlier in the evening.

"You brought me presents?" She couldn't believe someone could be so kind to her.

I kissed the Virgin on the forehead and she blushed a beautiful, bright pink all over.

"Yes, read these. You will learn so much about the world if you do."

"Thank you. I will."

"I can't stay here any longer, your father could come in at any minute."

"Wait..."

"Yes, princess?"

"I love you."

I always knew how she felt about me but for now, I had to pretend to think she meant it platonically.

"I love you too, princess...I will return when you finish those books."

"Okay."

I left her side and room quickly, leaving no trace of my exchange with the girl. From there I made it to my bed, stripped down to nothing and hid under the covers, safe from waking life.

Chapter Thirteen
The Temple's Womb
Number Three – The Astrologer

"Christian love has no place in the world we are planning to create. Marriage and monogamy are merely systems of control over women, and all variations in between. Bacchus celebrates love between men and women, men and men, women and women. Like Bacchus, we share our love until we become our love."
-Hersh, Number One, Lord Bacchus, Child of Love

I was naked on a bed of rose and lotus petals. My arms and legs were tied down by long tendrils of ivy. The smell and smoke of burning incense filled the air. I couldn't move and I was told not to speak. I was only allowed to breathe, moan, scream, and cum. I looked down the crest of my pregnant belly and saw my husband, the Thief, and the Magician sitting there, staring straight into the eye of my vagina. I looked up at the ceiling and through the gaping oculus could see a full moon.

"We must link sexual activity to the lunar cycle, it is the only way we will tap into the ancient knowledge within every cell of our bodies," Hersh said as he appeared over me for a moment then walked over to my husband.

Orgies or Marxist sex, as I consider it, promote gene mixing, higher birth rate, and communal responsibility for the children. Orgies are one of the few solutions to all the divisions facing humanity. Share your women because we want to be shared. Share your men because they need to be shared. There are less men than women born into the world and there are far less eligible men for women to deem worthy of mating. That vacuum of women that go without a good dicking should be filled with men living by a Bacchic set of principles that lets them fuck without consequence or guilt. That might sound patriarchal if you've never tried it but if you have, you'd know that group sex dissolves the male ego. Lack of sexual dominance and ownership over a woman would shake the power structure of the patriarchy until it totally topples. A Bacchic world cannot exist without orgies, it has been the keystone of the Festivals of Dionysus since ancient times.

"Number Four, you're first," Hersh instructed the Magician.

The Magician sighed and stood up, sloppily jerking himself off as he walked over to me. He kneeled down before my vagina and hesitated to insert himself. It seemed he was having trouble stiffening.

"What's wrong?" I asked, "You used to love fucking me..."

"Forgive me, I just need another minute."

He knelt there, with everyone watching and judging him. If he could not perform it would cause a rift between my husband and him.

"You can't take this long, just put it in me how it is," I whispered at him sharply.

The Magician exhaled and followed my instruction, letting his soft cock slouch into me as he vacantly thrusted over and over. He pretended to moan and groan and I wailed and flailed all about, trying to give the impression of really getting a good peg. Hersh and the Banker totally bought it and when the Magician pulled out and faked cumming in my mouth, they had no idea I had only swallowed my saliva and vaginal fluid. The Magician then returned to his place beside the Thief and Banker.

"You're next, Number Seven," Hersh instructed the Thief.

"No thanks," the Thief just shrugged.

"*What do you mean, no thanks?*" the Banker furled his brow at the Thief.

"Yeah, what *do* you mean?" he Magician seconded.

"I don't feel like fucking her anymore," the Thief grimaced.

Hersh laughed at the Thief's charming audacity.

"What's wrong with my wife?"

"She's gotten too fat and boring, my dick has no use for her anymore," the Thief explained.

"She's not fat...she's pregnant. And if not her, who will you fuck? You're not gonna fuck the Somm, *that dyke*."

"Nope, not her," the Thief shrugged.

"You're definitely not gonna fuck Inga."

"You're right, I'm not."

"You're not actually thinking about...my daughter...*ARE YOU?*"

"I didn't say that...I could easily go without fucking anyone, honestly."

"That's a very Apollonian thought, Number Seven... I won't stand for it," Hersh suddenly turned serious.

"I can't help how I feel, Hersh. I refuse to fuck the Astrologer."

"Fine, then I must make a decree, Number Seven...I give you the privilege of being first to take the Virgin in your bed."

"WHAT?" my husband nearly had a conniption.

I was excited about this turn of events though, I see how my daughter looks at the Thief. If there was anyone to take her virginity, it should be him. Let her fulfill her love at least once, before she's taken.

"Fine, if I must," the Thief sighed, rolled his eyes, and drooped in his seat.

"Who the hell gave you the right to give away my daughter?" The Banker shouted at Hersh.

"No one gave me the right. I am a God, Number Two," Hersh replied.

"You're the God of wine but you're not the God of virgin daughters. You cannot tell my Scarlet who is going to take her virginity."

"Why don't we ask her at dinner then? Let her decide."

"Yes, let her decide," I broke my silence.

My husband glared at me, "SHUT UP. You're forbidden from speaking, you fucking whore."

"You're forbidden to question a God," Hersh told the Banker. "I should punish you."

"Really? How?"

"No wine for you at dinner tonight. Everyone else can drink but you, you're going to be completely sober."

The Banker blushed, deeply embarrassed.

Chapter Fourteen
The False Spring
Number Ten – The Chef

"It's been a long and painful week and the weather isn't helping. My skin and mind are cracking. EVERYONE seems to be pissing me off...everyone except the Thief, who reminds me of myself, an eternal child. One thing's for sure, If I break, the Banker breaks too."
-Hersh, Number One, An Angry God

Little chickens living in total darkness twenty-four/seven. Little chickens on low-protein, near starvation diets. Little chickens, doomed to die, in a false-winter. The executioner turns on the bright factory lights for twenty hours every day and now the little chickens think winter has turned to spring. The false-spring and introducing high-protein diets forces the little chickens to lay eggs at a rapid pace, three hundred a year. That's two or three times more than little chickens naturally lay. After a little chicken's first false-spring they're usually killed because they never lay as many eggs the second year.

These are only the horrors that befall little chickens designated for egg production. The bigger chickens doomed to wind up with their carcasses on your plates and their flesh between your teeth, those big chickens face an even grizzlier fate. As terrible as their deaths are, their lives are just as bad. Take a tour through the killing floor and see baby birdies with their eyes crusted over, scabs and bald patches covering their bodies, debeaked with a searing hot blade. Does your blood curdle at the thought? If not, you're part of the problem.

Hormone-fed, genetically engineered chickens needed for meat are painfully plucked, have their heads pulled off then their feet removed. A vertical incision is made to open up their bodies so their guts can be scooped out. Often times, those guts will accidentally burst open and feces will spill into the bird, contaminating the meat. So, it reaches your plate and you eat hormone-fed chicken shit and get sick. For those who have experienced this, you got off light, I wish you choked.

My thoughts cross the suffering of chickens as I spoon some vegan mayonnaise into an "egg" salad filled with vegan algal based "eggs," cumin, onion powder, kala namak salt, tofu, curry powder, and chives. The "egg" salad is one of multiple sides for the evening including, rice pilaf with dried apricots, stuffed acorn squash, and the main course, vegan "meatballs."

I plated everything and brought it out of the kitchen, into the dining room. I set the plates all around the table for Hersh, the Banker, the Thief, and the Magician. All the men started eating, stuffing their fat mouths, teasing me as I walked away. I returned to the kitchen where the Astrologer, Sommelier, and Virgin were chomping on the leftovers that didn't get plated.

"Hope you're all enjoying everything."

"The egg salad is delicious," the Astrologer spoke while chewing.

"Try the meatballs," the Virgin suggested.

"Number Ten is about to get the Thief's meatballs in her mouth," the Sommelier snickered.

The Astrologer laughed at her daughter and the Virgin giggled, punching the Sommelier in the arm, making her howl with laughter.

"You're just jealous, bitch," the Virgin accused the Sommelier.

"In all seriousness, she is," I said.

Suddenly, everyone was staring at the Sommelier until she stopped laughing.

"*What?...*you think I'd *actually* fuck the Thief?"

"You say that like there's something wrong with him," the Virgin replied.

"Isn't there?"

"He's a fine young man, trust me," the Astrologer smiled.

"I'm not into the whole interracial thing," the Sommelier spat out.

"Are you fucking serious?" I couldn't believe her.

"Oh, does that make me racist?"

"Of course, it does."

"How? It's my business who I let penetrate me," the Sommelier defended herself.

"Dark-skinned men make incredible lovers, dear. There's no need to deprive yourself of all the wonderful varieties of dick in this world," the

Astrologer broke it down.

"I assume you're not a fan of Asians, Indians, and Jews either?" I asked the Sommelier.

"Actually, those ones aren't so bad," she replied.

"*pffft...*" I rolled my eyes.

"Whatever, I have to get out there with tonight's bottle," the Sommelier shrugged and walked out of the kitchen, back toward her cellar.

"I think it's time we go too, bring the little one to the boys," the Astrologer put her hand on the Virgin's shoulder and led her into the dining room.

Chapter Fifteen
Peter Pangender
Number One – The Hierophant – God

"Just because I'm an intersex God, doesn't mean I do not lust. Even at fifteen, I find myself alone in bed, touching myself and letting my mind be consumed with thoughts of my two crushes. The Thief and the Virgin... how I wish I could throw myself in the middle of them but alas, I could never confess my feelings for my lucky number Seven."
-Hersh, Number One, The Intersex Bisexual Bacchus

We all sat around the table, my friends and me. Scarlet's mom took her by the hand and walked into the dining room to join us. Scarlet looked really cute with pink bows in her hair.

"Gentleman, Bacchae, I bring you my daughter, Number Ten, the Virgin," Opal introduced her.

"Hi," Scarlet said, shyly.

I looked over at the Thief. He was smiling, trying to keep his tongue behind his teeth so no one could see him slobber. *My sweet wolf, of course Bacchus will let you dine upon her.*

"Number Seven, Ten, you both know why I brought you here. Number Ten, would you like it if Number Seven was your first?" I asked her.

She smiled warmly and looked into Jesus' eyes. He stared back with loving confidence and his charm began melting her to mush.

"Yes. I would like that very much," she nodded.

"Are you sure, dear?" Charles interjected.

"Yes," she turned to him sternly.

Charles leaned back into his chair and crossed his arms over his chest.

"Why him?" Charles asked.

"I think he's beautiful. I've always thought he was beautiful."

"Who else would take her virginity, Number Two?" I asked.

"I don't know...why don't you have a go, Lord Bacchus," Charles laughed at my expense.

"I've had more experience with love than you know, Number Two. Clearly you haven't read your mythology."

Just then, Mindy strolled into the room and up to our table with a bottle.

"Tonight's wine is considered the perfect wine. Southern Australia's Pensfolds 60A vintage 1962. It's a Cabernet Sauvignon and Shiraz blend that tastes like sun-dried plums."

She poured everyone a glass as Charles stared, hypnotized by the dark red liquid that would pool out of the bottle's lip into the glasses. When Mindy reached Charles, she lowered the bottle to pour into his glass and only but a drop came out before I raised my hand.

"Stop."

Mindy raised the bottle and looked up at me.

"I have revoked the Banker's drinking privileges this evening."

Charles raised his glass and let the one drop of Penfolds roll up the glass, into his mouth and down his throat.

"You can't revoke anything from me," Charles said to me.

"You're on thin ice, Number Two," I warned him.

I looked around the room and saw everyone taking sips of their wines.

"Alright, now that everyone has a drink, lend me your ears, I have a history lesson for you all. A lesson of all the loves I've had in my divine life."

Everyone perked up to listen except Charles, who seemed not to care and just kept eating through my lesson.

"I had divine loves and mortal loves, both men and women. My first goddess was Aphrodite, ever heard of her? That's right, the goddess of love picked me as her mate. She was intoxicated with me. After I got her pregnant, I thought we would love each other forever but alas, she found another before our son was born. As punishment for her promiscuity, Hera punished her by making our son, Priapus, hideously unattractive."

"I didn't know hermaphrodites could have kids," Charles said under his breath.

I blushed, terribly embarrassed then slowly simmered into furiousness when I looked around, realizing everyone could read my face.

I didn't pay Charles' interruption any lip though, I just kept telling my story.

"After Aphrodite was Aura, the virgin," my eyes turned to Scarlet, objectifying her as much as a child's gaze could. She stared back, totally under my spell. I knew then that having her was only a whim away.

"She was the titan goddess of the breeze. After I raped her, she bore me two sons, twins. The first twin she ate alive, she had resented me so. The second, Lakkhos, was rescued by the gods."

It was so silent, you could hear an eyelash bat, the Bacchae revered me.

"There were also many semi-divine nymphs that clung to me. There was Beroe, who left me for Poseidon. There was Kronois, who mothered Kharites, and there was Nikaia, a nymph I raped who then mothered our daughter Telete."

"You don't have it in you to rape, you're a dumb, innocent little kid," Charles murmured again.

I closed my eyes and took a deep breath. As quietly as Charles spoke, everyone heard him and was waiting for my rebuttal...but with tears in my eyes, I kept lecturing.

"There were also plenty of mortals. There was Althaia, who had another daughter of mine, Delaneira. Ariadne, the princess of Krete, who married me and gave me seven sons. There was Erigone, a maiden from Attika and Pallene, the princess of Pallen. Lastly, Physkoa, a votary of mine, who had my son Narkaois,"

"Lies, lies, lies, you've never fucked a woman in your life," Charles said, louder this time.

"SILENCE."

Charles smiled, delighted at my trauma, obviously laughing inside.

I then turned to Jesus, "There were also men I've loved in my life. Ampelos was a beautiful satyr, and Polymnos took me to the underworld and asked if we could have sex once. I came back but when I did, I found him dead. I then buried Polymnos and placed a wooden phallus upon his grave."

Charles belted out a brief chuckle. As soon as we locked eyes, he couldn't help but burst into uproarious laughter.

"How dare you laugh at me. I am a God. I should have you killed for this."

Charles kept laughing, banging his fist against the table and wiping tears out of his eyes. Everyone else was stone-faced and scared out of their wits with the exception of the audacious Jesus, who seemed entertained by the show that he cracked a smile against me. Cracking that smile cracked my mind and suddenly it was like I was the butt of the world's joke.

"Stop laughing. Fuck you. You're nothing. You're nobody."

As quickly as the snap of his fingers, Charles stopped laughing to speak.

"I'm nobody? I created you. Before me, you were nothing but an abused and orphaned child, abandoned by parents who didn't love you because you were a retarded freak. No one wanted you but me. NO ONE."

He struck a chord in me that hadn't been touched in years. With a sharpened blade, he stabbed that vulnerable place and forced me to cry.

"Stop, you can't talk to me that way," I meekly mumbled.

"The hell I can't. Where are your parents, Hersh? Why haven't they tried to find you?"

"I don't know, they must not love me," the tears were streaming down my face, I was blubbering badly.

"They don't and neither do we...do you honestly think they *LOVE* you?" Charles gestured at the rest of the collective, "FUCK NO. They *FEAR* you."

Charles laughed and I totally broke down.

"Not me though, I'm not afraid of you at all. I've seen you for all that you are."

"Stop. Leave him alone," a timid voice shouted.

I looked up and saw Scarlet lashed out against her own father.

"See what you've done, Hersh. You've torn apart my family,"

"It's not his fault, it's yours," Scarlet courageously continued.

"What I'm about to do to her, is your fault too, kid."

Charles stood up and slowly strolled over to his daughter. Every one of the men was too cowardly to stop him and even his wife was too brainwashed to disapprove. He got an inch from Scarlet and pulled his hand back, prepared to break that pretty face again. Before he could strike her though, I grabbed Salerno's glass of wine and broke the orb so that I could wield the jagged stem like a knife. I then shot up, onto the table and ran up to Charles then slashed him across the face. His warm blood splattered over me and he screamed, gripping his lacerated face in grotesque pain. He pushed me and I stumbled backward, hitting my head on the table. It hurt so bad I couldn't get up. Charles' blood spilt everywhere. The gash ran from above his right eye, over his nose, and to his left cheek.

Salerno and Jesus got up and grabbed both of Charles' arms, restraining him from coming for me.

"You might be able to hurt me, boy...but I can ruin YOU. Never forget what I did for you. Never forget where you were before me."

Salerno and Jesus dragged him out of the room. Scarlet came to my aid, cradling me and caressing my head like I was a baby again, in her loving arms. For that one moment of her touch, it was all worth it, even if it meant the beginning of the end for us all.

Part III
Some Are Born To Suffer

Chapter Sixteen
The Unholy Union
Number Eight – The Virgin

"Time heals all wounds. The banker's face, my broken heart, the Magician's faith, the Sommelier's constitution, all these things have been damaged, repaired, and transformed. After only a month and a half, it's as if we're not the same family. The only thing that's remains the same is the weather."
    -Hersh, the soon to be dead God

Leading my eye with my scrawling finger below the last sentence of *On The Origin Of Species*, a sickening feeling befalls me when I realize that I'm out of books to read. Having crammed all sorts of subversive truths between my ears over the past month and a half, reading till I drove myself quasi-mad, I have a whole new lease on life to thank the Thief for. Tonight, in front of my mother, father, and what remains of our Collective, I will finally give my body to him under a new moon. It's my hope that his penetrating me will disrupt the fates so powerfully it will shatter the Dionysian spell everyone is under into a million pieces.

My mother brought me a beautiful white dress to wear during the ceremony. It starts with a tight ring around my collar with white ivy crawling up my neck. A thin layer of white lace drapes down from the collar with an opening in the center, exposing my sternum, belly button, and beautiful, shaved pussy. It feels like my wedding day.

True love will kill the Collective. Faithfulness, loyalty, and honesty will all be nails in BDC's coffin. Maybe it's my naivety but after living in a place without any recognition of the nobility, dignity, and grandeur of the human spirit, love feels like a revolutionary act.

I get naked and then shackle the dress around my neck. I am nude but regal, my skin is pasty, supple, soft, and fragrant, like the inner-most flesh of a fresh pink petal. I brush my blonde hair and after the two-hundredth stroke there comes a knock at my door. It must be my mother.

"Come in," I instruct her.

She opens the door and approaches me. She is wearing a black hijab that illustrates the stars and planets.

"The moon is out and the collective is waiting for you...are you ready?"

"Yes."

My hair is sufficiently straightened, so I put my brush down and stand up.

"Should I follow you?" I asked my mother.

"No sweetheart, you should lead," she answered.

My little feet slid out of my quarters and my mother closed the door after us. The lights were turned off throughout the temple, only by fire was my way lit. I walked into the temple's main chamber where sweet fruits and flowers covered the floor to symbolize my virginity being swept away in a soul stirring storm of the senses. There were two small red pillows waiting for us on the floor, mine read "Eight" in gold and his read "Seven." So, I sat on mine and my mother left my side to take her seat with the rest of the Collective on the balcony.

My father watched me without a shred of disappointment or disdain, his eyes were cold and long past judgement. The wound Hersh shredded diagonally across his face healed into an equally grotesque quilt of mismatching skin. My mother sat next to him, gripped his hand and he wiped his leaking eye. The Sommelier walked over to father with a bottle of wine from the family vineyard and a glass. She set the glass down and poured him some to drink.

"Thank you, my dear," my father gently whispered.

"You're welcome," the Sommelier nodded.

My father's burning anger had been quelled by his scarring. The shame made him decent again. If he was still his old self, he would've already had a fit by now.

The Sommelier took her seat beside Inga while Hersh was sitting on a throne, decorated in ivy, with his legs spread open and member sticking out. He smiled at me when my eyes met his then he nodded, blushing.

"Now that the Virgin is here, I will play the Thief's introduction," Hersh exclaimed as he pulled his flute out from a crevice in his seat. He brought the flute up to his lips but before playing, he mentioned one more thing.

"This composition was written by Number Nine. It's called *The Farmer's Plow Bends Before the Autumn Harvest on a Cold Wedding Night*."

The song was minimalistic and melodic, if this was the sound of Bacchic marriage then it must be an odd, off-kilter form of love, one that is perhaps too lofty to pursue for an entire lifetime. Into our gathering, came the Thief, dressed in a white linen shirt and pants with his hair made into an elegant ponytail. A brown-boy cultured by the white bourgeoisie, dressed up as if he was being groomed to fuck the white patriarch's virgin daughter. My eyes were glued to him, this handsome man, my very own savage. I heard a coughing coming from the balcony. Looking up, I saw it was my father.

"You look beautiful, my sweet," the Thief said.

My gaze fell back down to the Thief and he took a seat beside me on his pillow.

"And you look handsome," I smiled, glowing.

Hersh lifted his lips off from his flute and exclaimed, "Now, Thief...*disrobe*." A second later he continued the music and my boyfriend started stripping down to his hairless brown birthday suit.

Once Jesus was nude and Hersh got a good, clear sight of his erect penis, the music stopped and the Thief laid down beside me and started caressing my cheek with the back of his hand. We stared into each other's eyes.

"May I kiss her?" he asked Hersh.

"What the hell are you waiting for? *Of course,*" Hersh answered.

A smile dawned upon the Thief's face, but it wouldn't last long before meeting my lips in a firm, forceful kiss. His lips melodically glided down the rims of mine and his teeth latched upon my bottom lip for just a moment. I lurched forward as he pulled back. His head floated down from my face and past my neck to my nipple which he bit through my dress, making me gasp. I've never been so wet in my life. In a brash move, he completely tore the lace of my dress off, leaving just a white collar around my neck like I was a dog. He started sucking on my breast like a leech, desirous of draining me of every drop of juice. He sucked with conviction, with teeth and tongue and passion. The Thief clearly had a true love for pussy, he was no pansy. Speaking of which, while my mind and eyes were elsewhere, one of the Thief's hands quickly snuck down my body to my pussy and rubbed it raw till I began gushing all over the floor. His body looked beautiful upon mine, there was a certain extra three-dimensionality that seemed to exist when his brown hand rested on my white breast. As my eyes rolled up into the back of my head, they quickly passed the sight of Hersh pleasuring himself intensely from the balcony.

"I'm going to cum. I'm going to cum," I shouted then came.

Convulsing on the floor, pushing the Thief away with my little monkey foot, I was splish-splashing in my own juices until the Thief sat up on his knees, pushed down my thighs, each knee pointing in a different direction, and exposing my vulnerable, pink pussy to every array of attack. His cock was massive, with vines of veins crawling up the shaft as it throbbed in anticipation of me. He spread my pussy lips with his fingers and my eyes snapped open to look at him.

"I want your dick inside me. I want your dick inside me now. Oh my God, fuck me. Fuck me. Fuck me."

The Thief forced himself into me and filled me up beyond any measure I ever imagined. Flat on my back now, I was being delightfully stabbed over and over. Staring up, I saw the peanut gallery, voyeuring and Hersh still masturbating. My Mother smiled beneath her hijab. My father looked totally stolid and dead inside, sipping at his wine, nearly at the glass' end. The Magician shied away, unable to watch this pornography. The Sommelier had her arms crossed over her chest, unimpressed. The Chef was actually sleeping.

"Ugh, ugh, you feel so good. Your wet, tight, creamy pussy feels so good," the Thief moaned in ecstasy.

"It's yours. My pussy is yours. It belongs to you," I shouted as every thrust arched my back up.

Suddenly, the Thief laid on top of me, covering my fulfilled frame. He kept pumping in this position, his chin buried in my shoulder. After a few more minutes of this, he came inside me and with him, I did a second time. After us, Hersh came too, his body folding like a woman but his spirit shooting out of him like a man.

Jesus' body convulsed, cramping on top of me until he raised himself off and pulled himself out of me. His cock was covered in vaginal fluid, semen, and my hymen.

"That was incredible," I said, feeling a new connection to my man.

"I'm sorry I didn't last longer."

"You lasted plenty long. We have all the time in the world to keep fucking...I never want to stop fucking you."

He smiled, and from the balcony, the violent sound of coughing caught our attention. It was my father, huddled over his seat and hacking up what could've been a lung, it sounded so intense.

The Chef woke up and looked over at my father, startled.

"Is he going to be okay?" she asked.

My father shook his head and croaked out a "No," through his incessant choking. Mother unraveled her hijab, revealing her face and started slapping my father's back, trying to expel the obstruction in his throat.

"Are you choking? Oh dear, I think he's choking."

Suddenly, a wave of blood sloshed out of my father's mouth and plopped onto the floor with a disgusting sound. My mother screamed and my father collapsed forward onto his face.

"Charles," she shrieked.

She knelt down before my father's body and spun him around onto his back. His tongue was sticking out of his mouth and his eyes crossed then went blank. A mixture of blood and wine covered him from his face to his belly.

"He's not breathing," her voice rang like an alarm.

"Do not panic," Hersh instructed us and stood up.

"What do you mean? My husband's dying."

"No, Number Three... your husband is dead."

"No...not yet, I don't believe it," she started performing CPR on him, frantically pushing air into his dead, empty chest.

"How did he die?" my boyfriend asked.

"By poison. Number Two is the one who must die by poison," Hersh affirmed.

"*Praise Bacchus*," the Sommelier added, pulling every eye and suspicion her way.

Chapter Seventeen
The Man That Would Be Queen
Number Five – The Sommelier

"Choosing who lives and who dies is no easy task, not even for me but to show difficulty in making the decision, that is a terrible offense in the eyes of a believer. I had no doubt the Sommelier killed the Banker."
- Hersh, Curious Child, God

The others all stared straight at me with daggers for eyes. A trail of blood trickled out the Banker's mouth and down the balcony, dripping to the floor of the temple where his daughter's bloody hymen had broken. Nonverbally accused of murdering my boss, words were necessary to plead my innocence but as watery as my eyes could well-up, it wouldn't be enough to garner any sympathy.

"Stare all you like, it wasn't me or my wine."

"You've always resented Charles...even though he treated you so kindly," the widow barked at me.

"Kindly? Excuse me, but none of you is an authority on kindness. Especially Charles. Don't act like this is some tragedy...let's be honest...who of you is not relieved by that bastard's passing?"

The Astrologer and her daughter gasped.

"Hersh, merciful Lord Bacchus, please. Do something. Let her suffer for my husband's death."

"I didn't kill him but I'm happy he's dead. For how he treated Scarlet, how he treated Hersh, and lastly, how he treated me."

"He treated me terribly," Hersh added, shaking his head.

"Wine would make him say and do crazy things, Lord. You know in his heart that he always loved you," the Astrologer pleaded with Hersh.

"Even still, he was the closest thing to a father I ever had," Hersh continued.

"Don't let him off the hook for all the violent things he did," I reasoned.

Hersh turned to me with tears in his eyes.

"Bite your tongue or I'll cut it off, Number Five."

Suddenly, a terrible, wrenching fear shot through me. I knew I'd be killed.

"If it wasn't for the Banker then none of this would be here. Without him, I would not be your Lord. Your insolence is no surprise to me though, I've come to expect it. Insolence toward me and of course toward your murder victim..."

"No, that's not true, I didn't do it."

"Yes, you did," the Astrologer butted-in.

"You did, Number Five, and you'll be punished for it severely," Hersh decreed.

"H-h-how?" I stammered.

"One must die by fire, one must die by frost, one must die by hanging, one must die by drowning, one must die by eating, one must die by being eaten, and one must die by lust. That's all that's left, do you have a preference?"

I looked at them, waiting for me to come up with my own means of execution but to their dismay, I decided I wanted to live. I ran for my life down the balcony, jumping one story to the temple floor below where Scarlet and Jesus were still naked. I landed on my feet and rolled my ankle but not even that excruciating pain could stop me.

"Get her. Murderer. *MURDERER,*" the Astrologer shrieked.

With every stabbing, painful step, I neared the temple doors until running behind me came the Thief, naked and determined to catch me.

"Don't do it, Jesus. Please," I begged him, nearly out of breath.

He didn't listen though, he didn't even respond. He wrapped both his arms, tightly around my chest so I could not escape. I tried kicking backward, hoping to knock around his exposed scrotum but it was no use. Within moments, the rest of the collective had circled us and though the Thief had released me, there was nowhere for me to go.

"Why did you do it?" the Astrologer demanded closure.

Trying to catch my breath, the lack of air to my brain made me feel rather lucid. I had accepted my end and thus had more clarity and sureness in my words.

"I did it for humanity. For the individual. Bacchus Death Collective will not get their way. The collective is now decapitated and rudderless."

"Charles was my inferior, not vice versa. I have always been our head and rudder," Hersh fumed.

"No. You and everyone else were just Charles' puppets and now the puppeteer is dead," I replied.

"Have you decided how you'd like to perish?" Hersh shot back. Reminding me of my death was his only comeback.

"Surprise me, you freak," I snarled.

"Strip her," Hersh commanded.

Suddenly, like a pack of wolves or flock of vultures, they descended upon me, tearing my clothes apart until I was in nothing but my underwear. I tried covering up my tops and bottoms with my hands but it was no use.

"Lust? You're going to fuck me to death?" I asked Hersh.

"Take off her bra and panties," Hersh commanded.

They were closing in on me with eager fingers until I put my hands out and backed them off.

"No, I'll do it," I said to stifle their advances.

I pulled down my panties and unstrapped my bra. My breasts and vagina were now seen by the collective's naked eye. A smirk dawned upon the Thief's face.

"Do your worst," I dared them.

Hersh smiled then turned to the Magician. "Number Four, escort Number Five out of the temple, down the elevator and out of the building."

"Yes, sir."

The Magician grabbed my arm and dragged me to temple's big doors. He pulled me out into the hallway outside where a security guard was sitting behind a desk, completely stunned at the sight of my naked peril.

"Can...can...can I help you?"

"Call the fucking police, they're trying to kill me," I screamed.

"Open the elevator, we're going to the ground floor," the Magician commanded.

"Yes, sir," the guard answered the Magician.

The security guard stood up, ran to the elevator behind him, swiped his keycard in the first lock then the second lock and pressed "G." As soon as we stepped in, the doors closed and the elevator slid down the side of the building.

"Look outside," the Magician said to me.

I stared out the glass elevator and saw the city was frozen over. Hail, snow, and rain were falling upon the dead.

"This is how they're going to kill me?"

"They won't kill you. The city will."

"One must die by frost...."

"It will be slow and terrible."

"There's no guarantee it'll kill me. What if I find shelter?"

"I hope you do. To Christ I hope," the Magician sighed.

"Can't you do anything? If you really feel that way."

"No," his eyes started to tear up.

I looked at him and truly saw Salerno for the first time.

"You don't seem as happy as the others over this."

"I'm not like them. I never was. I don't know why I let myself get so brainwashed. I'm sorry, Mindy. Please forgive me."

I gulped heavy, using a slice of my time of dying to feel sorry for someone else.

"I do," I said.

"Thank you, for killing that bastard."

"You're welcome. Had I seen this coming, I wouldn't change a thing," I smiled.

The elevator reached the bottom floor of the building and the doors opened. We stepped out of the elevator to the silent and empty lobby. Not a soul stirred for me to ask for help. The Magician walked me to the building's exit where a single security guard was standing. I ran to him and knelt at his feet, tugging his pants, crying, wiping my tears on him, begging, screaming, wailing.

"Please, help me, he's trying to kill me, call the police, for God's sake, please, I'm fucking begging you." My hysterics were met with just as much coldness in his heart as there was outside.

"I'm sorry, may God have mercy on your soul," the guard kicked me off of him and I fell backward onto my ass.

Crying, I stood up and fled out the doors into the city. The moment I stepped foot out there, I was assaulted by a brutal freeze. It was a needle through every pore of my body. I could see my breath with every pant. The Magician followed me out of the building but stopped at the entrance to call out to me.

"Thank you, Mindy. I promise your sacrifice will not be in vain. I will make sure the Collective falls apart and all Charles Gaiman's plans will come crashing down."

"Fuck you," I shouted back as I kept running into the city.

I found the body of a dead bum on the side of street. He had icicles dripping down from his nose. I tried taking off his coat but it was stiffly frozen onto his body. I left the body be and kept on running, hoping to find an open door or heart. I found nothing of the sort and just stopped at the next apartment I could find and started pounding on the door with all my might.

"Let me in. Let me fucking in. I'm going to die," I screamed.

Out of nowhere, a woman emerged from the second-floor fire escape and saw me below, in all my desperation.

"You. Open the door for me please," I begged her.

She returned back into her apartment and I panicked below her window. I was elated to see her reappear but out of nowhere, she dumped a bucket full of dirty mop water all over me. Its coldness felt like searing hot fire and I went into shock, running for my life. I would die within the hour, on a park bench, trembling and trying to absorb the heat of two frozen homeless corpses beside me.

Chapter Eighteen
Reinforcements
Number Four – The Magician

"The end is looming. It's as if the souls of all the people I've damned have floated down from the heavens to park over my head so they can have a front row seat to my demise. In this moment, I only wish I could see my mother again. I wonder if she'll feel my passing in her heart, I sincerely hope so."
-Hersh, God in the twilight of his humanhood

I watched the pale skinned Sommelier run down the street into the heavy white fog. I sighed and a cloud of hot air holding a piece of my soul escaped me. Perhaps that's all the fog was, a collection of a dead city's sighs.

"Christ," I bemoaned.

I hung my head and turned around, back inside the Gaiman Building. I eyed the security guard who kicked the Sommelier away and nodded at him.

"Thank you, sir," he said.

"I need you to unlock the elevator," I replied.

"Of course, sir."

The guard escorted me to the elevator and used his keycard for the outer lock. I pressed the top button for "penthouse" and climbed up the frigid sky like an angel upon Jacob's ladder. The doors opened up to the guard sitting behind his desk. I stepped out of the elevator and stood over him for a moment.

"Yes sir?" he asked.

"I told you the day would come when I'd need a favor, well, the day has come..."

"I'll help however I can."

"I need to use your phone."

"Yes, sir."

The guard handed me the rotary phone attached to his desk and dialed star seven to let me call any number outside of the building.

I took the phone's receiver and pulled the dial-pad over to punch in the seven digits belonging to my brother in arms, Chris Borden. It was late and Chris was surely sleeping but as fate would have it, nothing short of death would get in the way of me reaching him.

"Hello?" his voice creaked with tire.

"Chris. This is Sal."

"Are you serious? What time is it?"

"About four in the morning, I need you to pick me up from the Gaiman Building."

"It's freezing outside."

"Why do you think I need a ride? Otherwise I would've already started walking to you."

"Shit. Is a ride all you need?"

"Gather four other men to meet us at your home."

"My home? What will you need my home for? My wife and daughters are sleeping."

"We will keep our plotting quiet."

Chris groaned for an extensively long grog.

"I'll be there in twenty minutes."

"See you soon. I'll be out in front of the building."

I returned the phone to the guard.

"Give me your keycard for the elevator."

"Can't I just open it for you?"

"No."

"I can't leave without it. I could lose my job. I won't even be able to go home to see my family until you return."

"This is bigger than your job or family."

"Promise me you will return it."

"I promise."

The guard sighed, dug into his pocket to retrieve his keycard and handed it to me. I swiped it through the first lock on the outside of the elevator then through the second on this inside and pressed "G" for ground.

When I reached the bottom and the doors swung open, I scanned the scene for the guard. It was in both our best interests I remained unseen. There were cameras on me but at this hour, no one behind their monitors. I stepped out the elevator and bum rushed the entrance until the guard caught a glimpse of me.

"Sir, what are you doing down here again?" he asked.

"Oh, I left something outside after I left the girl."

"Really? What did you forget?"

I was never any good at thinking on my feet but was always a proficient bully.

"Fuck off, fat ass. I can't be bothered right now…don't you have anything more important to do?"

"The penthouse called earlier and said two people were coming into the lobby only once and only one should be leaving. They also said, if anything different were to happen then I should report to them immediately. So here you are, in my lobby for the second time. You might have disobeyed your instructions, but I will not disobey mine. So, I'm calling the penthouse right now, please cooperate with me and stay here without making a fuss."

"Cooperate with you?" I asked just before taking the bastard by surprise by pouncing on him and wrapping both my arms around his neck in a rear naked choke. Clenching as tightly as possible, I exerted every ounce of force in my arms to constrict the guard's windpipe like a boa. I could sense him waning in my death cradle.

"Let me go, mother fucker," leaked out of him.

"No. Wrong place, wrong time, wrong decision, my friend…now I have to kill you. You left me no fucking choice."

I kept choking and choking and choking him, lobbing around his body to dislodge any last bit of spirit still in him. His face turned from red to purple to blue to white. Finally, I sensed his finale and released him, dead on the ground. I checked his pulse and like his breathing, there was nothing.

Chris' car came barreling through the roundabout outside the Gaiman Building's entrance. I saw his headlights glaring through the glass doors as he honked a few times to call my attention. I lifted the dead guard under his arms and dragged him out the doors with me. I couldn't just ditch him for anyone to find, there could be no trace of my leaving.

The sight of a dead body being lugged to his truck shocked and infuriated Chris for being dragged into my mess.

"What or who the hell is that? *Is he dead?*"

"Yes. Help me put him in the back of your truck."

"Fuck, man."

"No bitching, Chris. There's gonna be plenty of bodies by the time we're done."

Chris' dashed hopes to continue bitching were let out in a sigh as he exited his truck to help me hurl the guard's body back into the flatbed. Once the corpse was secured, Chris and I jumped into his truck and he peeled out of the driveway so fast you might have thought the building was about to come crashing down.

"It's so fucking cold out, why the hell did you have to get out tonight of all nights?"

"Because Charles fucking Gaiman died tonight."

"WHAT? *How?*" Chris couldn't believe it.

"Choking on his own blood, after being poisoned by the only decent human in the whole lot."

"They still let you out of the temple?"

"Because someone had to escort the bitch out into the cold so she could freeze to death."

"Geez, you people are sick. I can't imagine a worse death than freezing."

"Yeah right, I can think of plenty."

"Maybe you're right. Why'd you ask me to call four other guys? You know how pissed they were for having to wake up at this hour...and why the hell do we need to use my house?"

"I'm going to show you what magick is face to face tonight. Because we're going to participate in a ritual."

"A ritual? For what?"

"To cast a spell on the brotherhood of righteous men that will make us strong and lucky enough to put an end to the collective."

"I don't know...I'm a Christian. Using magick doesn't sit well with me."

"I'm a Christian too, man but this must be done."

"You don't think putting on a ritual is sacrilegious? I don't gotta kill no babies or anything, do I?"

"No one will get hurt but yes, it is sacrilegious and thank God it'll be the last time I ever have to do it. That said, we're going to need a few things in order to cast the spell correctly."

"Like what?"

"Cinnamon, salt, chalk, candles, a knife..."

"That all sounds easy to acquire."

"Then also a goblet and a baculum."

"I probably got a goblet but what the hell is a baculum?"

"A penis bone found in large animals."

"Where the hell are we gonna find one of those?"

"Maybe you know someone."

"I got some big friends but not that big."

"No, I mean someone with access to one, asshole."

Chris and I were splitting at the sides. It was the first time I had genuinely laughed in such in a long while. I almost started crying.

"Oh, and one more thing."

"What?"

"I need a white hooded robe."

"Why white?"

"White for benevolent magic during a waxing moon."

We found a nearby dumpster and tossed the guard's body then drove into Brooklyn until arriving at Chris' house where we waited for the others.

~ * ~

We had the basement to ourselves. I was wearing a white bathrobe over a white Yankees hoodie with the hood flapped over my head. In white chalk, I drew the magick circle and pentagram with every point touching a candle. After drawing the Qabalistic Tree of Life in the pentagram's center, I started consecrating the circle by sprinkling salt, cinnamon, and sulfur-rich gunpowder around the border.

"Everyone get to your positions," I commanded.

"Chris and the four other men he gathered stood at each point of the pentagram."

"This is some freaky ass shit," one of the men sneered, making everyone but myself break out in a chuckle.

"Magick is supposed to be taken seriously, your life and death hang in the balance."

After that, no one dared take the moment lightly.

"Who of you have the baculum?"

The surliest of the men, Roy, stood at seven feet tall with a long grey beard that fell over his tattooed barrel chest. He reached into his jeans and pulled out a blunt tusk-like bone, still with bits of blood and flesh stuck to it.

"Where did you find this?" I asked.

"Wrestled a bear," Roy smiled.

"Hmph...save the story for drinks after we finish."

With everyone in position and the circle consecrated, I took the knife and baculum into each hand and raised them over my head as I stood in the circle's center. Without a book of conjurations, I depended solely on memory and the authenticity of my heart to utter the right words and avoid the disaster of another botched ritual.

"In the names of the many Gods of the many worlds, I put my life in your hands to aid in the banishing of Bacchus from this realm. I invoke my father, protector of Solomon's temple. Please Father, empower us with your benediction that we may defeat our enemies in battle, for they are the enemies of man. I invoke thee, armored and winged Godhead."

I set the baculum in the fire pit and let the animal's blood melt off the bone and seep into the coal to feed my father's summoning.

"Your wings burn a brilliant gold and your hair is as black and vast as the night sky. Rise from the dead to bring a final death to all those that evil men have resurrected. Once dead, always dead. Once perished, always perished."

I closed my eyes and projected my own spirit above me. There I waited, sitting with my legs crossed, for the angel of my father to visit me again. After a few moments, there he was in my mother's arms. It was a De Palma family reunion.

"We're proud of you, Salerno," my father informed me, his eyes shining a brilliant and honest blue.

"So, I have your blessing to complete the ritual?"

"Yes," my mother said. "This will redeem you of all your transgressions. Slash them and they will bleed out your sins, my son," she finished.

I snapped open my eyes and gripped the knife tightly.

"Everyone take your candles and step into the circle in front of the fire pit."

Everyone took four steps forward and arrived next to me around the fire.

"Everyone put out your right hand, palm open, facing up."

They all stuck out their right hands, palms opened upward. One by one, I slashed their palms diagonally, crossing their life-lines.

"Now reach into the fire and grab a coal then repeat what I say and release the coal," I let the severity of my instruction sink in for a moment then continued. "God of war, god of death, god of destruction, I am you. You are incarnate in me. Bacchus will be banished by your blackened hand! *For YOUR blackened hand...is MY blackened hand.*"

Each of them grabbed a coal in their bleeding palms and the sound of sizzling flesh filled the room only to be hushed moments later, under their chanting.

"God of war, god of death, god of destruction, I am you. You are incarnate in me. Bacchus will be banished by your blackened hand. For your blackened hand is my blackened hand," they all repeated.

"Now blow out your candles."

Everyone blew out their candles and I grabbed a bucket of water that I hovered over the fire pit.

"In this darkness, we end our weakness. In this darkness, the ritual ends."

I doused the fire out and in pitch black darkness, we waited in silence until I stepped out of the circle and flipped on the light switch. Now embraced by the light, I took off my hood.

"You got anything to drink, Chris?"

"Whiskey."

"Good."

"So, what now? Are we gods?" Roy asked, skeptically.

"There's only one way to tell," I answered.

"How?"

"Punch something."

Roy clenched his blackened fist, focusing all his power into his hand. He then swung his tree trunk of an arm and connected the front of his blackened fist into a concrete wall. He cratered it so deeply that it sent shock waves up his arm that cracked the skin up his wrist. He pulled his hand away to examine it closely, dumbfounded as to how he felt no pain.

"There's only one God and it ain't any of us...that said, whatever power you gave us, Sal, we're gonna use it to give this world back to the people," Roy said, staring at his hand in a cold trance.

~ * ~

We were driving into Manhattan when the sun came up from behind the steel ridden horizon. Chris' hand was still stained black, not by ash but by magick. Chris dropped me off in front of the Gaiman Building just when every employee was arriving for work. If being seen leaving by one security guard in the middle of the night was bad then being seen by hundreds of employees in the busiest moment of the morning meant I was completely fucked.

I immediately caught every stare on my way to the elevator. By my dress and demeanor, security must've assumed I was a homeless that wandered out of my bounds.

"Excuse me, sir, are you in the right place?" one guard asked me.

Without saying a word, I pulled my keycard out of my pocket and swiped it through the elevator's digital lock. It opened and embarrassed, the guard showed no resistance against me stepping into the elevator without answering him. Before I could swipe my key into the second lock and press the "penthouse" button, a wave of employees flooded into the elevator with me until it crowded to the brim. One scrawny old man in a suit was pressing everyone's buttons for them until every button was lit but mine.

"Penthouse please," I asked him.

Everyone's eyes veered a bit toward me, wondering what an elite was doing among them, but the scrawny old man showed no shame in asking.

"I've worked in this building twenty-six years and never once have I seen anyone get off on the penthouse."

"So?"

"So, I hope you don't mind if I ask what goes on all the way up there?"

"We sacrifice virgins to the Roman God Bacchus," I replied.

The old man let out a fake chuckle while the rest of the scared-shitless sheep stood there, awkwardly silent. As soon as the elevator arrived on its next floor, everyone poured out to let me have the ride to myself. When I arrived at the penthouse, the temple's guard shot out of his seat to confront me.

"Excuse me...sir," the guard eagerly spat as if he had been waiting just for me all those hours.

I kept walking to the temple, paying him no mind.

"My keycard, sir...I need it back," he begged.

"I'll be back," I told him.

"Shit," he cursed to himself.

Kissing those doors to gain entrance, I returned home to an empty temple because those that live in praise of Bacchus love sleeping in.

Chapter Nineteen
Picking My Brain Like A Lock
Number Seven – The Thief

"With all this death and sorrow committed by the Collective, one might lose sight of the good we are responsible for. Bonded together for the rest of their short lives, the Virgin and the Thief are the most beautiful thing I've ever created, they're the best kind of lovers this life produces, young and doomed."
-Hersh, Father of Aphrodite's Child, God of Drunken Sex

Rusted diamonds refracting elemental shadows. The spectrum of light isn't half as vast as the spectrum of darkness. Darkness comes in every shade and all are found in the deepest core of my cavernous heart. Wrapped around that dark core, sealing it like it were a dirty secret, are walls too thick, sturdy, and tested to ever penetrate.

I stroll through a gallery of paintings of all the women I've ever fucked hung up on eternity's walls. Each painting is for sale and sells to a collector and that collector is me. The Virgin is my latest acquisition.

It's not until I blink that I realize this is one of those dreams where I am in total control of my body and the setting it's in. I blink again and I'm lying in bed beside Scarlet. I blink again and I'm back home at my parent's little shack in Guadalajara. I can hear the clucking of chickens and barking of dogs. The air is pungent and musty. My mother is sitting at our kitchen table peeling carrots over a bowl of orange shavings. I sit down at the table with her and she doesn't even notice me.

"Mama?"

She doesn't respond or look up, she just keeps peeling her carrot. Which, upon closer inspection, is no carrot at all but a wooden phallus she's whittling. She shaves down the shaft and engraves the creases of the head. I swallow hard and look back into her eyes.

"Mama, *mirame. Estoy en Casa.*"

Nothing. Perhaps she's gone deaf since the last time I was here. That was fifteen years ago. I snap my fingers in front of her face and out of nowhere, she bites my finger clean off. I scream before waking up beside Scarlet then fell back asleep to mulligan my dreams. This time I asked myself, what do I want to do after this is all said and done? Where do I want to be once the temple is in shambles and the Collective are all dead?

I transported myself to a deep, blooming forest far away from mankind. Immediately, my ears were ringing with a medley of hums and chirps made up of perfectly synchronized animal mating calls. I suppose that's how unobstructed life-force should sound. The air was clean and crisp, the trees were every lush shade of deep green, and the sky was as blue as Aryan irises. In every direction and in every moment, there was an outpouring of growth, always changing. Compared to this, the cities are the static on your TV screens. See and hear the white noise of death, it's calling for your heart behind that thin square of glass. Here, I felt shielded from reality by taking shelter in my dream. I wondered if like a dream, nature too will vanish, and we'll wake up to something far more concrete.

I was smiling in my sleep until I felt a stabbing pain in my rib. I opened my eyes and saw Scarlet trying to wake me with her elbow. She was crying.

"I had a bad dream," she told me.

"Really? About what?" I asked.

Chapter Twenty
If Lovers Shared A Mind
Number Eight – The Virgin

"A woman's mind secretes stories like they were endorphins. For every love, she crafts a story. For every story, there must be an origin, stakes, and a resolution. The dreams she dreams while in love are like flowers she gives herself."
-Hersh, Drinker of Dreams

Heaven and hell sleep side by side, sharing a mattress. In between, well I guess that's purgatory.

"I dreamed you died as sacrifice to Bacchus," I told Jesus, sobbing.

"Babe...there's no need to cry about that, it's what we want. Isn't it?"

"I don't know anymore. I'm confused," I confided in him, blaspheming.

"Only one of us will survive anyway, chances are it's not going to be either of us with Hersh stacking the deck in his favor."

"I don't want to die. I'm only eighteen years old."

"If that's what you want, you'll live, babe. I'll make sure of it, even if it kills me."

"NO. That's even worse, Jesus. How am I supposed to live without you? I'm in love with you. Even *thinking* about being without you hurts so much. That's why I'm crying."

"*Shhhhh*...you think too much, babe," he said, wrapping his arms around me.

His face must've been only an inch from mine. He smiled so sharply I couldn't help but smile too but only for a second before wiping my tears.

"I dreamed you were eaten...it was horrible."

Jesus just laughed like I knew he would.

"Did I taste good?" he asked.

"I don't know, I wasn't the one doing it."

"Don't know why they didn't eat you instead, you taste great," he joked then playfully chomped away at my arm.

I giggled...*what a beautiful idiot.*

"Get the fuck out," I joked then Jesus pulled away.

"Who was eating me in your dream?"

"There were dozens of people in the temple. Destroying it. Smashing the statues. Burning the paintings. Killing us all. They ate you but left me alive to watch."

"Who were they?"

"All men of all races, all in their forties it looked like."

"That's it? You don't remember anything to identify them by?"

"There was one thing..."

"What?"

"Five of the white guys had black hands."

"Like black skin?"

"No, like charcoal black."

"Hmph..." he thought to himself for a minute. "That's troubling."

"Why?"

"You've got a lot of psychic power, Scarlet, even more than your mother."

"I hope you're wrong because if what I saw ends up happening, then we have to leave this place today."

"We will..." he yawned.

There was a dull moment between us that convinced Jesus to close his eyes.

"First let me just get another hour of sleep," he submitted.

"What if...."

I sensed him fading away before I could reply. Only the strong can sleep in the face of terror, so at least that brings me some shred of calm.

Chapter Twenty-one
The Oracle
Number One – The Hierophant – God

"If one could only see the future then there would be nothing left to fear. That's why the Banker and I have been hiding the future because once they see it everything will make sense. Nothing makes Bacchus sicker to his stomach than making sense."
-Hersh, Merciful God of Madness

I make sure to wake up early, put on a clean robe, and slip into my slippers. My days are numbered, so every moment is sacred and deserving of a ritual. I step out of my quarters and trot over to Jesus' room. I open the door quietly, without bothering to knock. He's in bed with her. They seem happy and they should be. They lived and died admirably in their final days.

"Jesus."

Jesus snapped awake.

"What the hell, Hersh?" he asked, startled.

"You can't talk to him that way, Jesus," Scarlet told him.

"Fine, forgive me, Lord Bacchus, why the hell are you here?"

"I want to show you something."

"It can't wait till after breakfast?"

"No."

"Alright, I'll be up in a minute."

He laid in bed showing no signs of stirring.

"I'm sorry, Jesus. Perhaps you misunderstood me. I want to show you something right *NOW*."

Scarlet smacked him across the chest and he sighed and sprung out of bed, naked. He walked over to his pants that were strewn on the ground and pulled them on.

"Do I need a shirt?"

"You didn't even need pants."

"Guess I'm ready."

"Follow me."

I skipped out of Jesus' room and together we strolled through the temple to Salerno's door. I knocked three times and waited for a response.

"Why would you knock on his door and not mine?"

"Well, there's a chance he's not even in."

"What makes you say that?"

"He might've flown the coop...*again*."

"How did you know he once tried?"

"That's actually what I wanted to show you."

Suddenly, we heard a muffled commotion from inside the room.

"Just a minute," Salerno shouted from inside.

Instead of waiting for Salerno to gather his bearings, I decided to push open the door and catch him in the act. There he was, still dressed in the same outfit from the night before.

"Good morning, Number Four, what time did you return last night?"

"Late."

"Did you get lost in the building? Have trouble finding the exit?"

"No, I'm afraid the Sommelier put up a bit of a fight."

"Really? The guard wasn't able to help you?"

"Guard? What guard?"

"Well, can you at least confirm she's dead?"

"No. How could I without following her? You'd have to send someone out into the city to find the body."

"You wouldn't be interested in the job, would you, Number Seven?"

The Thief's face fell blank.

"*Never mind*... no point in wasting time. I'm sure she's dead. I woke you and the Thief here because I wanted to show you both something special."

"Alright, show me."

"Come this way."

I walked out of Salerno's door and down the hallway. Salerno and Jesus dragged behind me and with keen hearing, I eavesdropped backward, listening to them trying to wrap their heads around my supreme omniscience.

"The fucking kid just told me he knew you tried running away,"

Jesus told Salerno.

"He must have people on the outside. I bet he knows about all the trouble I got into last night too."

"Right this way, friends," I said as I pulled open the door to my quarters.

I led them inside, right up to my surprise for them. It was draped in a black cloth that fell plainly over its spherical head.

"This is it. Behold."

I pulled the cloth off and revealed the glass orb beneath. The orb was held within the grasp of an onyx dragon's claw sculpture.

"This is the Oracle."

"It shows you the future?" Sal asked.

"It shows me every future, every present, and every past, all I have to do is ask."

"So, you've seen all my transgressions?"

"No need to worry, I forgive you. Not that my pardon matters where you're going."

"Why should we believe you?" Jesus asked.

"Poor Number Seven, I really pity you. As I've known all along, you don't believe for a second there's anything special about me."

"You're right but don't take offense. I've been through every crevice of this continent's underworld and seen every con there is. Religion, of any stripe, is without question the most antiquated of those dopey tricks. You're not a God, Hersh. There are no Gods. There are only people and animals. Charles Gaiman was nothing more than a snake oil salesman and you were the oil."

"Oracle, show me a God," I asked the Oracle.

A milky white smoke swirled inside the orb. As that smoke saturated into a deep fog, from out that fog appeared my face. My face then grew older and my hair turned black and I grew a beard. I had become Bacchus.

"You don't think I was chosen by Charles only for my unique genitals, do you? He asked the Oracle just like I did."

"If this thing shows you the future, have you asked it who will die?" Salerno butted in.

"Long ago."

"So, every time someone's been killed, you've known it would happen?"

"How else could I have passed judgement so quickly? We knew the Somm would order hemlock with her wine, weeks before she even did. Charles wasn't crying because his daughter was being given to Jesus...he was crying because he knew it was his last day on Earth."

"Show us our fate. If you can really see the future, show us both our deaths, you false God," Jesus put his foot down.

"Not without a please," I smiled, batting my eyelashes.

"You won't do it, because there's no truth to any of this."

"Fine. I'll cut you both a deal."

"Here's a deal, you fucking freak, why don't you take that poor excuse for a cock between your legs and stick it in that Godless snatch beneath it. Sal and I will get the fuck out of here and you will rot all alone like you deserve. How's that for a fucking proposition?" Jesus shouted at me, livid.

Jesus then flipped me off with the double bird and started walking backward to the door, "Come on, Sal...let's go."

"You won't make it out of the city alive. The fate of the collective is sealed and all are flawlessly finished off but one."

"The one is you, right?"

"Want to find out? Whomever of you kills the other gets to see the future."

Jesus laughed, "You really think we'd go for that? We're friends, man."

"What if my future shows me dead? Is there anything I can do to change it?" Sal asked, much to Jesus' chagrin.

"Nothing at all," I assured him, my smile curling like a fish hook.

"I can't believe you'd even ask," Jesus turned to Salerno, coldly.

"You're so closed-minded, Jesus. You don't want to believe in magic? You want to call all the miracles I've seen trickery? I've cast spells and spoken to Gods that could devour your soul with the snap of my fingers. There are more than humans and animals on this plane, alright. There are things that keep gods awake at night. So, I believe Hersh when he says his little toy has taught him how to play with our lives."

"Everything you know was taught to you by one cult or another, Sal. You never developed your own truth. So, I'll do you a favor and tell you the answer you've been groveling for...we control our own destinies. That was the fatal flaw of this collective in the first place. We should've been building our world in our own images, not in the image of some narcissist."

"I won't kill you, Jesus. Don't you worry," Sal said to him.

"Wonderful. I'll be going then, to my quarters to get my woman and out of this temple forever. Goodbye."

"Before you go, there was something I wanted to show you in the Oracle."

"I don't want to see my future."

"Not the future. The present."

"Don't bother, I'm sure Sal is still brainwashed enough to give a shit, not me though."

He strolled right out, leaving Sal and I in a very awkward tension.

"Didn't expect that, did you?" Sal asked me.

"No, I saw it in the Oracle."

"Yeah right, I can read it all over your face...you can't believe someone finally denied you."

"You think that's the first time?" I laughed.

"In the temple, it is."

"It's no matter, so I've lost control of one of my sheep," I shrugged. "It's too late for him, anyway."

"You've lost control of two, not one."

"You're right, the Thief has stolen the Virgin from me."

"Three then. Myself, the Thief, and the Virgin."

"I haven't lost you, Magician. I have you right where I've always had you. Right under my thumb," I pantomimed crushing him under my thumb.

"What if I decided to kill you right here? Beat you to death with my bare hands? Punched your skull until it caved in and your eyes were buried in a heap of shattered bone?"

"You won't."

"How do you know?"

"Oracle, give the Magician an update on what our children are doing."

"Our children?"

"The demons we created in that botched ritual."

The Oracle fogged up again as it conjured up another film for us to watch.

"Before Charles died, he instructed his people on the street to initiate a chain of events that would make the city a more fertile place for

Bacchic madness to seed. As soon as we all die, those seeds will sprout."

The first image to appear in the Oracle was of dark green ocean water under moonlight. It was like we were the eyes of a bird flying inches above the sea. Below us, the tide was flowing forward because we were flying away from the mainland and to a distant obelisk sitting in the fog. The closer we approached this obelisk, the sharper its image became until finally, we realized it was Rikers Island. Our bird's eye flew onto the island and through a wall into one of the prisons. It traveled down a dark and quiet cell block and just stood there for a moment. In the time it takes to let out a long, desperate sigh, an explosion of fire erupted at the end of the cell block. A barrage of flames, smoke, and debris came shooting at our bird's eye and we slowly hovered toward the source of the explosion. The floor was covered in shattered concrete as we arrived at a gaping hole in that wall. From the gaping hole, dozens of masked men in black uniforms with assault rifles stormed into the prison. Each of the uniformed men ran to the door of a different cell and pulled out what looked like a miniature lightsaber which they switched on to open a searing hot blade that they used to burn through each cell's lock. Once the locks had been ruptured, the uniformed soldiers opened the cell doors and uniformly stormed right out the way they came. The cell doors stood still and open until slowly, from each cell, stepped out a naked woman. One by one, their eyes burned red with inner inferno. They walked and growled as if they were feral.

"The daughters of Lillith, remember them?" I asked Salerno.

"The women that killed their first-born boys," Salerno couldn't forget.

"Our children."

"That's your plan? Releasing them to unleash more suffering? More Death? What else is new?"

"Keep watching...it gets more interesting."

The Oracle's eye followed what seemed like one hundred women out of the cell block and through the hole in the wall. Once they were all out of the building, the woman looked up at the crescent moon and shrieked with piercing howls that rang all the way to Manhattan. Little boys and girls miles away woke up in their beds, screaming and crying. From out of the backs of these bitches, grew black and fleshy bat wings. Living gargoyles, these women became, shooting into the air and gliding over the ocean and into the city to wreak havoc.

"They really are demons now, Number Four."

"I don't believe it. I won't. Prove it, you rotten little brat," the Magician spat as he gushed hatred my way.

I simply pointed up and his eyes followed my finger to the Oculus in the ceiling of my room. After a few seconds of staring up at the sky, one of these demon women flew right past the window, showing us her ugly underbelly.

"Jesus suffering Christ," the Magician was in awe, this was too vulgar a display of magick.

"Keep watching, you don't want to miss a moment of this," I said pointing back to the orb.

The Oracle followed the demon spawn through the city. Grabbing people off the street and flying off with them to devour their heads. Flying onto fire escapes and breaking through windows to snatch babies out of their cribs to eat. Commotion followed the creatures everywhere they flew. Down below them, people would run for their lives, screaming, and cars would come careening into each other trying to escape. One demon perched atop a church's cross, heckling at the people down below until out of nowhere, a gunshot rang out through the night and a bullet blasted through the monster's chest. The damned soulless thing then fell to the sidewalk, dead.

"It seems people are fighting back," I shrugged.

"There are more good men than demons."

"They won't stay good if they're pushed to the edge. Charles' plans haven't even begun, keep watching."

Suddenly, the miniature Manhattan appearing in the orb turned dark. A rolling blackout. All the city lights turned off in a flash. Darkness spread over the land and with it came a chorus of terrified screams. The only lights left on were those in the Gaiman Building, shining like the Christmas spirit at the deepest, darkest ends of winter.

"We've seen enough, Oracle. Thank you."

Just like that, the Oracle faded to black.

"You cut the power off for the whole city?"

"Yes."

"People will freeze."

"If they want to feel heat they ought to dance or fuck," I laughed.

"You won't be laughing for long, Hersh."

"Will you stop me? Will your brotherhood of righteous men? When do I get to meet them?"

"Any minute now."

"You're so funny, Number Four. Going from one collective to another...just like the Thief said. Can't you think for yourself? The Thief doesn't seem to have that problem...and look how far it's taken him. He was just a poor Mexican farm boy."

"The Thief only cares about himself; he would let you destroy this world so long as he got off the hook."

"Will you be joining him on his way out?"

"No. I'll be staying right here. With this."

Out of his pocket, the Magician pulled out the elevator's keycard.

"Does that belong to Carlos outside?"

"If that's the guard's name then yes."

"Then the Thief won't be going anywhere after all. He'll be stuck here with us when your mob arrives."

"Good, he's just as deserving of judgement as any of you."

"Awww...you're a bad friend, Number Four. A Judas. You know what happens to betrayers, don't you?"

Chapter Twenty-two
A Thief Without A Virgin
Number Eight – The Virgin

"This is the part I've been looking forward to least, when our little family gets torn apart. Some will be killed in the temple and some in the streets. Some in the west, others in the east, and so on. I feel better knowing we'll all wind up in the same place in the end but it's just a shame that after investing this much time and energy into everyone's dying, I won't even be able to sit back and watch the fruits of my labor."
-Hersh, Tragic Figure

After Hersh took Jesus out of bed, I went back to sleep to dream of a post-Bacchic world. Life after all this drama climaxed and concluded with nothing more than a fairy's whimper. We were living on the family farm over in the Finger Lakes. Jesus, my husband at this point, was out in the vineyard, harvesting grapes with our workers. The sun beat down on their brown brows and made them forget any memory of the winter's brutality. Despite the heat, it was a beautiful day. I was sitting on the porch with a book, smoking a cigarette. I opened the book to the first page where Jesus had written a message to me. It read "Get up" with his signature under it.

Suddenly, I smelled a strange vapor. Curling my snout with every sniff and snort, I turned to my left and saw a bronze haze rising up from the manure lagoons out by the slaughter house. It was coming this way, a cloud of pig shit with indiscriminate hate in its heart. I returned my eyes to my book and flipped to its first page which read over and over, *"GET UP."*

"Get up," shouted Jesus, forcing me awake.

My heart rattled in my chest as I groggily watched him get dressed and grab his few belongings.

"Finally, I thought you were already dead for a second there," Jesus joked.

"I was having such a good dream...until the end...what are you doing?"

"Packing. We're getting out of here, babe."

"Didn't I tell you we should go like two hours ago?"

"You're damn right you did and I'm sorry that I didn't listen, NOW PACK YOUR FUCKING SHIT."

I stood up and grabbed a dress and jacket to wear, quickly jumping into them. Jesus picked his jacket up from the floor and reached into its pockets. He then pulled out a photograph and stared at it begrudgingly.

"Fucking aye," he said to himself.

I saw three people in the picture, probably a mom and dad, with their kid it looked like. I didn't pay much attention to it, an heiress needs to concentrate while packing.

"You ready?" Jesus turned to me.

"Babe, I haven't even started."

"You're not taking any more than that. We need to travel light. We're going by foot."

"Babe, my clothes are worth enough that we could sell them and use the money to start a new life."

"You think people are gonna buy your clothes? People out there hate you, babe. They recognize you. They despise any Gaiman's face. We need to be fast and talk to as few people as possible."

"Jesus, you're being unreasonable..."

"We can't waste any more time."

He grabbed my hand and forcefully pulled me out of the room. I didn't bother resisting, my stuff wasn't as valuable as my man, even if he was an ass.

He took me to the temple's main doors and kissed them softly, seducing them to open. For the first time in two years, I left the temple and the world became larger by one hallway. We walked down that hallway to where a security guard was sitting at his desk.

"Gimme the elevator key," Jesus commanded the guard.

"I can't, sir."

"What do you mean you can't?"

"I'm sorry, sir but your friend took it."

"DAMN IT...*Sal*...what if there's a fire or something and the elevator doesn't work? Isn't there an emergency exit?"

"There's a staircase at the other end of the hallway."

Jesus turned around and saw the door.

"It only opens from the other side," the guard continued.

"What. Why?"

Jesus just sighed and wiped the stress off his face until we saw the elevator start descending from the penthouse down the building.

"Why's it leaving?" Jesus asked the guard.

"I don't know. Someone must have requested it from the ground level."

I read many emotions on my lover's face. None of which concerned me but worry. Jesus never used to sweat anything, but now, he was a stone's throw away from trembling.

"Jesus?"

He flinched and turned to me, "What?"

"I'm scared."

Part IV
The God of Death is Dead

Chapter Twenty-three
The Invasion
Number Seven – The Thief

"Man cannot handle power. No matter how righteous their heart begins, power corrupts it evil. Everything you know and see is a product of corrupted power. The only antidote to power is Bacchus, who by drink and dance can make anyone relinquish it."
-Hersh, Corrupted Christ, Seat of Divination

I have always considered myself part feline. Like a cat, a thief must keep his nine lives in pocket, never knowing when one will have to be sacrificed to keep the rest intact. Also like a cat, I've always been able to sense danger coming and something about that elevator being summoned by some outsider who wanted to come up to the temple, didn't sit well with me at all.

"Jesus?"

"What?" I asked Scarlet.

"I'm scared," she said.

I grabbed her hand and held it tightly.

"I am too," I told her.

She started breathing heavily. I could feel her pulse quicken through the throbbing veins in her hand. We stepped over to the e levator's locked glass doors and peered down the edge to see the capsule stop at the bottom floor. After an eternal minute, the elevator started lurching back up to us.

"Shit...it can't just be one person," I reasoned. "A few had to pile in there."

"They're here to kill us, aren't they?" Scarlet asked, fearful and tearful.

"We're sitting ducks here," I concluded. Scarlet reasoned correctly.

We turned around and walked toward the temple doors, but before we could reach them, the staircase door at the other end of the hallway burst open to dozens of men, hollering and howling and chanting together, holding all sorts of weapons. Burning torches and cold steel, sharpened axes and polished baseball bats, rifles, handguns and every firearm in between, in the hands of good men hell bent on destroying evil.

"Enemies of humanity. Prepare to meet your death. Enemies of God. Repent before you die," the mob chanted uniformly.

Scarlet screamed so terribly when she saw them, that she froze and wouldn't budge to hide back inside the temple with me. She was crying hysterically, breaking down under impending death's tangibility. Only feet away from us, those with weapons to swing pulled them back to deliver their death blows, while those with firearms cocked and pointed them at our heads. My life started flashing before my eyes, and I was so disappointed by what I saw that I had to pause the movie and find a moment of clarity behind my closed eyes. Far away from this place in that total darkness, a brilliant idea came to me that I could save our skins, and as if my hand and mouth were being manipulated, I took my fist and laid it flat against my chest.

"The forces of darkness will never prevail and the Brotherhood o f Righteous Men will never fail," I shouted, loudly and proudly.

I waited a moment and noticed I didn't get killed or hear Scarlet scream. I opened my eyes and saw the mob had been tranquiliz ed. Their weapons were frozen over their heads until they finally just lowered them to their sides.

Suddenly, the elevator opened behind us and out came pouring another mob led by Police Chief Merle Swanson. This mob was just as big as the one in front of us but was composed primarily of police.

"Enemies of humanity. Prepare to meet your death. Enemies of God. Repent before you die," the police chanted.

They came after Scarlet and I with their weapons but before their bullets could mow through our flesh, the first mob called out to them.

"Brothers, do not harm them. They are on our side."

"*Are you sure? They look like devil worshippers to me*," one of the cops asked.

"*He spoke the Brotherhood's maxim*," another man informed them.

"*If anyone touches him, they get a blade up their ass*," another defended us.

From up the stairs came a third slew of men, this group led by Chris Borden and four others with blackened right hands. In Chris' left hand was a black baseball bat with Derek Jeter's signature engraved in gold.

"What are you all waiting for?" Chris asked the mobs.

"We found a man outside the temple," the mob informed Chris.

Chris stormed over to us and luckily, recognized me from the Longbow.

"Jesus Madrid. The Thief. Good to see you again," Chris exclaimed, jovial before the atrocities he was about to commit.

"Chris. Please, tell your men to stand down."

"Don't you worry. No harm will come to you, Jesus, I assure you," he informed me, then turned to his mob. "This is a good man. He poses no threat. He's with Sal."

"What about the girl?" shouted a voice and suddenly I felt a stab of fear drive right through my chest. *She was about to get off the hook, you fuck,* I thought.

Chris glanced down at Scarlet's terrified and crumpled body and with his finger, lifted her chin up to get a closer look.

"Scarlet Gaiman," Chris said, sending a murmur of death threats through his mob.

"Keep this one close by and don't take your eyes off of her," Chris instructed his men before separating us and throwing her to them.

She yelped and screamed as the men passed her around, handling her like a pack of wolves share a fresh baby deer.

"Right this way, princess."

"Stick with me, Scarlet, I'll take good care of you."

"Don't you worry, miss Gaiman. You won't have to pay for all the terrible things your family has done to us. Right boys?"

The mob cackled horribly at Scarlet, who was scared straight out of her own body.

"Leave her alone," I shouted.

The men shut up to see who dared take offense to their raping her, but once they realized it was only little ol' me, they kept their fondling hands on Scarlet until Chris decided to step in.

"Do not hurt the Gaiman girl or I will personally stick this bat up your ass," he shouted at them, tightly gripping his ebony baseball bat.

Like shamed dogs, they stood down and hung their heads at their master's order.

"That's the temple right there, isn't it? Those doors?" Chris asked me.

"Yes."

"Come right this way, men," Chris walked over to the temple doors and kissed them. Salerno must've told him everything about us. The doors didn't respond as Chris had hoped though, it appears that the temple only spreads its legs for lovers true of heart, meaning members of the Collective only. Wanting to penetrate, he didn't back down, in fact he became more aggressive and with a monumental punch with his blackened hand, he broke right through the doors with super human power. Once opened, the barbarians passed through the gates, into the temple.

"For God and Country," Chris shouted while wielding his bat.

He led the men in storming the temple and like liquid into a funnel, they all poured in through the doors. I found myself at the back of the mob without being able to watch over Scarlet in their violent clusters.

"Scarlet. Scarlet," I shouted.

"Jesus. Jesus," I heard but could not see her.

They ransacked every room they passed through, every piece of pottery and sculpture was toppled and shattered. The paintings were torn out of their frames, all the plants were uprooted, stamped upon and trampled over, any furniture was ripped to bloody pieces. There was no respect for the sacred among them.

"Scarlet. Scarlet," this was getting out of hand and I needed to find her NOW.

"Jesus," her screams came from ahead but not a pale limb or strand of her blonde hair was in sight.

"Where are you?"

There was no response. They must have shut her up, but I kept calling for her.

"Damn you to hell, you animals," I shouted, much to the amusement of these soulless jackals.

Fire was the inevitable first step to the Collective's deconstruction. Every corner of every room must be set ablaze. The first fire, in this first room began as modestly as a candle but soon grew into a sweeping inferno. The mob spilled out of the temple's burning foyer, down the hallway that led to each member of the Collective's quarters.

Arriving first at the dead girl's room, the mob broke into the Sommelier's quarters, breaking every bottle of wine they didn't drink. The madness of this mob's creation was so intense it had to be softened with a buzz that could detach them from this Earthly hell. Ancient and new wines, reds and whites, good and bad wines, dry and sweet, tannic and crisp, all were mixed together as they spilled from the Somm's cellar onto the floor in a crimson flood.

The Somm's room was adjacent to the Musician's, their next destination. Old instruments from exotic countries that he used to serenade the Collective with were hung up on the walls like art. The tornado of killers reduced those instruments into broken strings and splinters. The Musician's Stradivarius wasn't recognized for the treasure it was, or who's hands it passed through, when one cop stamped through its neck, choking the life out of it.

Next was the Chemist's laboratory and the fools of this mob, which were the whole lot, made the mistake of not taking caution with the death devices, kill-switches, and toxic chemicals the Chemist had been keeping. They started destroying everything indiscriminately, like a bull in a china shop, breaking beakers and bottles filled with all sorts of poisons and drugs that released hallucinatory and noxious vapors. Half of these cave men got sick and the other half started tripping. Those that got sick couldn't tell if they were drugged and that were tripping couldn't tell if they were poisoned. *Was this high dying or is this dying a high*? they asked themselves.

The sober lot that stayed clear of the Chemist's quarters were busy raiding the Magician's and even though none ever stepped foot inside, just by the look of its contents, they could tell the room was Sal's.

"Where's Sal?" Chris shouted.

"He's with Hersh," I shouted back, as I made my way to Chris at the front of the mob.

"This is his room, isn't it?"

"Yes."

"These books..." Chris lifted up one of Sal's arcane tomes, "These are his magick books? Correct?"

"Yes."

"Good...BURN EVERY PAGE OF EVERY BOOK," Chris ordered our brothers.

They raised their weapons and cheered. Flexing their group-think, just as Chris wanted, every page of every book in the library was set ablaze. All the shelves of every wall were emptied that the pile's flames may touch the ceiling. Scarlet's screams traveled through the air but were sucked into the fire until the crackle of burning knowledge was all anyone could hear.

"Jesus, Jesus, I'm right here," Scarlet shouted, but like a train heading to an extermination camp, there was no going backward.

Soon the room would fill with smoke and we'd be forced out, so all hope of reuniting with her in this moment was lost.

After the Magician's room had been reduced to ashes, the mob set their sights on the Banker's quarters. The largest room in the temple, it was shared between the Banker and the Astrologer, yet she was oddly missing. So, without a human being to torture, discretion was pointless. Everything was burned. Her books, their clothes, and all his money. Not a single dollar was pocketed, it was all burned to hell.

The temple was beginning to fall asunder, but it wasn't until the mob made its way to the kitchen that they found a beating heart in a warm body to punish. At first, simply turning the knob to the kitchen's reinforced steel door didn't work. The power of the many concentrated into one force and attempted breaking down the door with everyone pushing at the same time. STILL the steel would not give. Police Chief Merle Swanson took the reins and decided only he could solve this problem.

"Stand back brothers. Let the professionals handle this."

Swanson led a few cops with a battering ram to the door and the mob cheered, their spirits lifted with the knowledge we'd indeed get to feast on who or what was inside. The boys in blue did their best, but even after a few good reams, the door wouldn't budge.

Our final hope, Roy the grey bearded giant, stepped forward. His blackened hand's blackness worked its way up his entire arm and so he simply pushed the door open with his shoulder, causing the massive steel doors to fall at the mob's feet.

The men stormed the kitchen, boots over tile, completely trashing it, demolishing all the plates, utensils, silverware, and appliances. Opening the fully stocked fridge, the men started throwing all the food and drink everywhere. Covering the kitchen like a drugged-out Jackson Pollock painting. Eventually, after checking every crevice, the squeaking and shivering of two bodies was discovered inside a mountain of potato sacks, stacked on top of them. The Astrologer and Chef screamed as the men reached into the pile, pulled them up, and threw them to the dogs.

"No, no. Don't fucking touch me. I've done nothing wrong," screamed the lying Astrologer.

The Chef, on the other hand, didn't seem as terrified, "Kill us. We deserve it. For all the evil we've done," the Chef solemnly admitted.

"That's right, you fucking deserve this," one man shouted.

"The fat one first. Murder her. Murder her," another followed.

One member of the mob grabbed the Astrologer while another grabbed the Chef, restraining every limb of theirs.

"How would you bitches like to fucking die?" the man holding the Astrologer shouted in her ear.

"Please, please...I beg of you. I'm a God-fearing woman, I'm pregnant with my second child, I...I...I've done you no wrong," the Astrologer cried.

"DON'T TOUCH HER."

Everyone turned to see who had shouted and saw their leader, Chris Borden, slowly stroll over to the Astrologer.

"Till I say so...*Don't touch her till I say so*," Chris smirked.

He then knelt down and with his blackened hand, picked up a big handful of pasta that laid at his feet.

"Please...mercy," the Astrologer pleaded with tears streaming down her face.

"Do you think we're stupid? We did our homework. We know you. We know what you've done," Chris told her.

The Astrologer kept silent, too scared to reply.

"Say your name, you fat pig."

Again, the Astrologer kept quiet.

"Here, I'll help you...O...O...O..." Chris tried to pry the name through her lips.

"O...O...O..." Stammering, she was unable to spit it out.

"Opal Gaiman, your day of judgement has come," and with that, Chris Borden stuffed the handful of pasta into the Astrologer's mouth.

"There you go...eat...chew...swallow...you don't want to choke." Chris grit his teeth as he shoved the food into her face.

The Astrologer's muffled whimpers beneath Chris' black hand only seemed to fuel his sadism.

"Here, you still look hungry, piggy," Chris snarled as he reached down and grabbed a whole head of cabbage. He ripped off a big chunk, too big for her mouth but still, he somehow found a way to cram it in. She screamed as his force-feeding snapped her teeth under the pressure and the cabbage disappeared between her cheeks.

"Shut up...don't scream...you knew this was coming...you will be murdered, slowly and horribly," Chris barked with his hand clutching her throat.

"Fwey hyu groff," she begged for her life through a mouthful of blood, bone, and food.

"Everyone, grab a piece of food and make sure it goes into Opal's stomach. Feed her until she bursts. When she can no longer eat, cut her open and stuff her like a turkey."

Chris released the Astrologer's throat and she fell to the ground at the mob's feet. Everyone picked up a piece of food and began crowding around her as Chris walked out of the circle.

"Borden. Wait," Swanson shouted at Chris.

"What?" Chris turned around.

"What about him?" Swanson pointed to the Chef.

Chris then looked over at me.

"Jesus."

"Yes?"

"Which one is he?"

"She's the Chef," I answered.

Chris turned back to Swanson, "Don't harm a hair on his body. We're taking him to the farm."

A few men grabbed the Chef and pulled her away.

"Kill me. Please, kill me," the Chef bemoaned.

"Don't worry, brother...you'll get your wish," one of the men assured her.

Chris led us all out of the kitchen, back into the temple's commons where smoke was billowing up from all of the pillaging we'd done.

"Have you found the child, yet?" Chris asked another man with a blackened hand.

"Not yet," he answered.

Then as the men carried the Chef away toward the temple's exit, Chris turned to me and grabbed me by the shoulder.

"Where is he?"

"Who?"

"Hersh."

"Probably in his room."

"Show me."

I looked down upon his hand as it rested on my shoulder and realized that now, not only was his hand black but the blackness had spread like a disease up his entire arm. He didn't seem to mind though, he was blinded by hatred. I swallowed hard and nodded.

"Follow me," I told him.

I led him and three other men with blackened arms toward Hersh's quarters, staring straight ahead until I heard her voice.

"Jesus."

I turned around and saw Scarlet, carried over the shoulder of the giant with the grey beard. His blackness had spread all the way up his neck now.

"It's you...thank God...are you hurt?" I ran to her and the giant set her down before me.

"Something cut my face," she said before embracing me.

Once I embraced for an eternal moment, I pulled away, held her face gently in my hands and brushed away a strand of hair to look closer and see that half of her face was covered in blood.

"Who did this to you?" I demanded to know.

Chris stepped over to me and with his black arm, plucked me off of Scarlet and turned me around like I was a ragdoll.

"That isn't important, Jesus. Is the child behind this door?"

"Yes, and now that you have him, there's nothing you need Scarlet and me for."

Chris chuckled, "Don't sell yourself short, Thief. We need you both. Neither of you are going anywhere."

When Chris opened the door to Hersh's room, he saw the God that had tormented him all this time, standing there, without menace. Some of his men started laughing...*all this fuss over a child?* they thought, but Chris was frightened of the boy, he felt the evil in the room enveloping everything. The Magician was there, too, indifferent to Chris' arrival or the temple's destruction.

"You must be Christopher," Hersh said.

"Salerno, has this foul creature hurt you?"

"No, I'm fine."

The Magician walked over to the mob and joined us. Hersh just stood there in all our crosshairs.

"What is it you want from me?" Hersh seemed more curious than frightened.

Chris didn't respond. He found any dialogue with Hersh, who he perceived to be demonic, to be potential death. Instead, Chris just ran toward Hersh and swung his Derek Jeter signed ebony baseball bat horizontally at the boy, aiming for the side of his skull. Without flinching, Hersh ducked just at the right time, as if he was possessed by angels of evasion, and Chris sent the bat directly into the oracle's glass orb, shattering it. From out the orb's core, rose a murky smoke that televised various images in its body as it moved. Images of Jews in Auschwitz were seen for the first time in color, Agent Orange's brutality upon Cambodian peasants, a black slave being whipped by a white man on a Southern plantation, Genghis Khan in a harem of Mongol hookers, and finally we saw an image that only myself and Hersh would recognize, Hersh as a baby being cradled by his Mama.

"By killing me, the only thing you will accomplish is removing the only trace of divinity in this world. Everything else is logical, material, visible, and without mystery...until I came along and unlocked the invisible world of magick that surrounds us."

"God doesn't need to be visible. It's my faith in him that ensures me I am justified in killing you. No matter how much you scream or bleed, little boy, in my heart I know I am doing God's work," Chris proudly told Hersh.

Hersh laughed at the big, brawny, jock turned killer.

"Go ahead and try, my work is already done. When I die, your God dies too and the pornographic symbol of his victimhood upon the cross will be replaced with the blissful symbol of a young boy, with blonde curls, dancing with women and a bottle of wine."

"Pornography? You dare smear the name of my God with such foul language? I'll show you pornography." Fuming, Chris then turned to Scarlet. "Bring the Gaiman bitch over here," he commanded his men.

"No," I shouted.

Roy, the grey bearded giant shut me up with a stiff punch to the stomach. His cudgel fist hit me with such a paralyzing bolt my feet fell from under me, and I came crashing face-first to the floor. My brain was feeding me every natural sedative so it could prevent me from seeing this next display, but I refused to slip into the darkness. I needed to see what they would do to my Scarlet. What I saw didn't seem quite real though, so I could've lost consciousness and dreamt up this whole thing. She tried to run but the giant grabbed her and carried her over to Chris.

"Brothers with black hands step forward," Chris instructed the men.

The giant and three others came to Scarlet's side.

"You were wrong, Hersh. You are not the only trace of divinity in this world. My brothers before you have all been marked by forces far from natural."

Chris raised his arm up and suddenly his blackened skin spawned ebony scales all over his body, covering him from head to toe. All the hair on his body shed and fell to the floor then his eyes took on a more reptilian shape. The faces of these demons began to transform more drastically, their mouths and noses erected forward, long like an alligator's. Then their eye brows turned to ridges and their foreheads grew long and flat and crested. The final transformation was of their fingers. First, the nails grew out and capped over their fingertips then they sharpened and calcified from enamel into bone. Emanating off the bodies of these five black reptilian demon brothers was some sort of black force-field that danced like fire off their bodies. Now this gaggle of fiends was standing over my Scarlet with evil intentions.

Blinking slowly, every other second was consumed in the total darkness behind my eyelids. The other men of the mob were scared out of their wits and realized they were no longer battling on behalf of good. They ran for the hills, out of Hersh's quarters, leaving Scarlet without anyone to protect her.

As soon as Chris tore off the front of Scarlet's shirt, revealing her breasts, she fainted backward into one of their scaly embraces. Hersh strolled away from behind the demons and over to the Magician, as if there wasn't a thing he ought to worry about.

"Let me guess, Number Five...you had some hand in this?"

"This wasn't supposed to happen..."

"You always say that...can't you create anything pleasant?"

The demons began raping my Scarlet. Their grotesque members defiled her every orifice and shocked her body into total numbness until no amount of pain was able to wake her out of her coma. Blood and fluid trickled down from their demonic union, pooling on the floor beneath them. The final death blow occurred when the demon that was once Chris Borden penetrated her with his ravenous demon cock. He was deep inside her and had flexed his member to claw and ravage into her insides. The one who must die by lust was indeed my Scarlet.

"Praise Bacchus," hissed the demons as they continued their assault on the dead.

"It was supposed to be a holy spell," the Magician bemoaned, hanging his head.

"No spells are holy when you're cursed, Number Four. You made the same mistake when I surrendered my body to you."

"Well, I won't be doing you anymore harm. It's been real, Hersh, but now I must be on my way," said the Magician as he casually sulked out the door.

Hersh sighed and watched him leave then turned to me and walked over to my side.

"Fine mess you've gotten yourself into, Number Seven. Never put someone else's life before yours, that's the lesson in all of this. You're lucky I've always had a soft spot for you. Come on, let's go."

Hersh kneeled down and with all his might tried pulling me up to my feet. He wasn't strong enough to lift me up himself, but he did inspire me to get up and carry myself out. As we left, the demons were still hard at work and showing no signs of slowing. Hersh and I dragged ourselves through the temple past all the fire and destruction.

"Such a shame that all our beautiful art had to be destroyed...these Christians don't even know how to pillage," Hersh shook his head.

We reached the gaping hole which was once the temple's entrance and exited our home. We turned to the elevator and saw the Magician and the security guard taking it down. With only a nod, the Magician bid us ado and descended down the building. We turned to the stairway to discover its door was wide open.

Giving my pain no mind, we pressed on and with twenty stories to go, we kept our minds off the brutal task of walking.

"Hersh, I have something of yours," I said as I reached into my pants pocket and pulled out his baby picture.

"Ah, I was looking for this...don't they look like lovely people?" Hersh asked.

"No. Not to me."

"Why not?"

"They look fake. Their smiles. Their clothes. Their hair. They're far from lovely...they're ugly."

Hersh didn't know how to react, perhaps though my love was tough, it was still at least love.

"Here...I want you to have this," Hersh reached into his robe and pulled out a few folded up pages then handed them to me.

"What is this?"

"Open it up later."

I slipped the pages into my pocket and just before we reached the bottom, Hersh turned to me, with a look I had yet to see on his face. A confused mix of shame and adoration.

"You know, since this might be the last time I ever see you, I have to admit I've always fancied you, Jesus. Perhaps in another life, where I was fully a woman, we could have loved each other."

"There are no other lives, Hersh, and if you understood that, you might've treated this one more preciously."

When we finally reached the staircase's bottom and opened the door, we walked into a packed lobby. The mob had gathered there, most likely waiting for us because the Magician and Chef were already in their custody.

"Get them," commanded Police Chief Merle Swanson.

Suddenly, a squad of police swarmed onto Hersh and I to separate and restrain us.

"Do what you will with the child and the tranny. Jesus and I are your brothers," the Magician pled.

"You're not my brother. Look what you did to Chris Borden. You're the worst of the lot, De Palma and you'll be punished as such," Swanson answered him then walked over to the front of the lobby to address the entire mob.

"Alright men, it's been a successful raid, we got everyone we needed. We're finished here, consider yourselves winners and whatever happens to this hell hole after we leave, good riddance. Feel no guilt. We are not responsible for any unforeseen harm done. No more half measures. Now throw De Palma, the tranny, and Jesus in the back of the van... As for the boy they call god, he's coming with me. Understood?"

The mob replied with a collective "YES," and Swanson simply replied "GOOD," as he turned around and exited the Gaiman Building. We all followed him out as the Magician, Chef, and I were escorted to a police van. They opened the back doors for us and we climbed in to sit along the walls. They shut the doors, entered the front end of the van and started the engine. The radio turned on with the car and played smooth jazz as we drove away.

We had no idea what to say, we felt like distant strangers from each other and ourselves. We were exhausted of all fury, pain, sadness, and fear, like human husks, trembling and cold. We had driven far enough to see the Gaiman Building fleeting behind us in the distance. Catching us off guard, the muffled sound of a single explosion came from the building's base and in an instant, the whole thing fell straight down into itself. A blast wave of dust and debris shot out and shook the van. Within moments of the cancer's removal, the city's power was restored and all the lights that were shut off in Charles Gaiman's grand plan suddenly came back on in one giant rebirth.

"Which do you think you'll be?" The Magician asked.

"Which what?"

"The one that dies by hanging, the one that dies by being eaten, or the one that dies by drowning?"

"Don't forget about the one that survives," I added.

"No, do forget about them. Hersh survives," he assured me.

"Really? With a record for being wrong like yours, hell...my odds just got better."

The Magician hung his head, accepting of much deserved disrespect.

"I hope I'm eaten," the Chef interrupted.

We both turned to her, not quite sure what had short-circuited in her mind.

"Inga, don't you see it was all bull shit? Hersh? The Collective? None of it was real."

"For all that people have done to this world, the least I could do is suffer," she replied coldly.

The Magician and I rolled our eyes then the van slowed down, came to a halt, and was put in park. We peeked through the little square portal windows on each door to see we were parked in the middle of Times Square. Suddenly, the doors opened and the cops that had driven us violently pulled out the Magician.

"You're first, the rest of you sit tight and watch," the cop ordered us as he pulled the Magician out onto the street.

They escorted him over to a giant mobile crane that was parked in the middle of Times Square. At the crane's tip was hanging a long piece of rope that looped into a noose at the bottom. Upon seeing that knotted loop, it became abundantly clear what they had intended for the Magician. A hooded executioner stood at the foot of the crane and pulled a lever to lower the noose an inch away from the Magician's face. The cops pulled his hands behind his back to handcuff them then the executioner wrung the noose around his neck and tightened it.

"Any last words?" asked the executioner.

"Mother, father, forgive me, please."

The executioner nodded beneath his hood and pushed the lever back. Slowly, the Magician was lifted off the ground as he kicked his dangling legs for dear life, desperately trying to break free in every impossible way. Finally, after putting forth a solid effort, his life had been choked out of him and was released into the same dimensions he corresponded with using his magick.

The cops dusted off their hands and strolled back over to the van and shut the back doors in my face. Then within seconds, they were back behind the wheel and driving away. I kept my eyes glued to the window watching the Magician's body dangle in the air, getting smaller and smaller. Like a symbol of salvation, the snow melted, the doves chirped, babies blushed, flowers bloomed, and all the pain the Collective caused came to an end.

The daughters of Lilith were stabbed by the searing rays of March's sun. The female demons kept to the skies, trying to fly away, had their wings burned to a crisp until they free fell directly to their deaths. The male demons who raped and killed my Scarlet would be soul sucked by the sun. The bodies of their former human selves lay like raisins in the light, naked beside Scarlet's corpse. Then once they woke up, retaining memory of their lives but not of the deeds they did the night before, they looked around the room and slowly realized what sins they had committed. Having broken every Godly law they ever held, the men didn't hesitate in killing themselves.

I had faith I'd survive this to see what new world would be born out of this existential and literal rubble, but I looked over to the Chef and could see she didn't share my hopeful disposition.

"Sooo...eaten huh?"

She didn't respond and though I was hoping for a dialogue to pass the time, thankfully, I remembered the pages Hersh gifted me. I pulled them out of my pocket and unfolded them to discover it was a handwritten suicide note written by Number Nine, the Musician.

Chapter Twenty-four
Suicide Note
Number Nine – The Musician

"For a musician, Number Nine was always quiet and kept to himself. He used to play concerts for thousands, gracing stages with magnificent charisma and initiating every audience into Bacchic revelry. It's a shame he had to take his own life, but I realize escaping his mortal prison on his own terms was the best option for him."
-Hersh, Suicide Solution

I love life but living here ain't living. I'm sorry to all my friends and family, my mom and dad, please forgive me, I've shamed you. You would've never seen this coming, I was a happy guy thrust into a place where there is no happiness, holiness, or music. I spent my life making beats and rhymes that made people happy, filling arenas with fire every night. I made men and women fall in love. I made tough guys cry and broken girls find hope. What do I tell my fans now? I'd tell them always to trust your gut and never take a dirty check. That's how I wound up here in the first place, taking money from people I didn't know or trust. I just trusted money. I thought I could trust myself but I couldn't, I was greedy.

I never had kids, I never found true love, and the longer I stay here, the more the ideas of those things get poisoned. When they die, I'll be a walking zombie. I don't want to live that way, I couldn't if I tried. All the music I make now is sad, weak and filled with apathy. The soul has been sapped out of me. Hersh gathered people who thought they were too good for life but he knows they ain't too good for death. If this note gets out of this temple, take my advice, live modestly and make something that will last forever because someday we'll all be gone, some of us before we're even laid to rest. Do not cry for me, cry for the world I helped create. It's coming and you won't know it's there until you wake up one day wondering where all human decency has gone. When that happens, if you kill yourselves too, I won't blame you.

Sincerely and with all my love, Leroy Rich

Chapter Twenty-five
A Sunday Morning Drive To The Ocean
Number One – Hierophant – Hersh

"Before I meet my end, I am destined to meet my beginning. The gap in my memory that aches my empty heart will finally be filled by a man who was instrumental to my meeting Charles Gaiman and becoming a God. If I die today then I at least I'll go somewhere I feel I belong. I've never felt at home here on Earth, anyway."
-Hersh, God of wine in this life and the next

When Police Chief Merle Swanson pushed me into the back of his police car, there was already a guest of his sitting in the front passenger seat to greet me.

"Hello," the guest turned around and said.

He was bald with a clean-shaven baby face and a white collar around his neck.

"Hello, priest," I replied.

Merle took his seat and got situated before putting his key in the ignition and starting the car.

"You don't remember me, child?" The priest looked into my eyes through the metal grating that separated us.

"No. I'm afraid I don't."

"That's funny, I thought you knew everything," Merle said before revving up his engine, kicking the car into drive, and taking us on our way. He didn't need to turn on his siren, the streets were as dead as they've ever been and totally belonged to him.

"My name is Father Roger Bacon. I remember you well, Danny," Roger began.

I swallowed hard, "That's my name?"

"Yes, child...the name your parents gave you."

"How do you know?"

"When your parents, Luke and Petunia, came to me—"

"What's my last name?" I interrupted, having to know.

"Vaughn."

"Daniel Vaughn," I said to myself.

"Doesn't sound like a pansy's name to me," Merle interjected.

"Your parents only ever called you Danny," Roger informed me.

"Luke and Petunia Vaughn," I whispered. "Are they coming?"

"Who? Your parents?"

"Yes, my parents, who else?" I shouted, starting to sob then fell back, feeling like an arrow shot me through the heart and stuck me to my seat.

"You think I'd want them to see what became of their child? Absolutely not."

I wiped my tears and sniffed up the river of mucus leaking out of my nose.

"If they didn't want me then, why would they want me now?" I asked my sorry self.

"I don't blame them," Merle chimed in.

"Can you take me to see them at least? Before we go through with this...?" I asked.

"What do you imagine is going to happen right now? You think we'd drive you all the way to Long Island to park outside their house and wait for them to come outside just so you could get one look at them? We're not here to fulfill any last requests."

"I don't know why I even asked," I relinquished all hope.

"I'll fill you in on what happened since they threw you away like garbage. They had one more kid and lived happily ever after, completely forgetting that you ever existed."

"They never asked about me? Not even once?"

"They would've come to me...but they never did."

"Why not?"

"They thought you were some kind of curse. That you were the work of Satan."

"Because of my hermaphroditism?"

"Yes, Danny."

I started blubbering all sorts of unintelligible sounds.

"That's where I briefly come into your life...I didn't have as big of an impact on you as Gaiman, but here I am again to tell you the tale."

"Why'd you come back?"

"It was Officer Swanson's request."

"I was only instructed by our mutual dead friend," Merle told us.

"Gaiman's hand seems to have been in everyone's pocket," Roger shook his head.

"What did you do for me, priest?"

"When your parents made the difficult decision of letting you go, they brought you to me at the Cathedral in the dead of night and handed you to me wrapped in a blanket. I cradled you in my arms and cooed you to sleep. Your pale skin was as cold as ice...freezing."

"Why are you telling me this?"

"Because when you don't know your past, you have trouble understanding who you are in the present. If you don't even know your parents' names, you can believe something as crazy as being a Roman god."

"I see what you're getting at."

"Good, so after your parents submitted you to me, I tried to house you in the orphanage, but the sisters felt uneasy about someone with your condition residing among the other children."

"You don't want a demon infecting all those beautiful little angels," I reasoned.

"That's exactly how they thought, I won't lie to you. I thought it was a very callous and un-Christian decision...*how I argued on your behalf...how I fought for you, Danny...*"

"You did?" My voice rose to a higher pitch, in disbelief that a wretch like me could be shown compassion.

"So, do you know what I did then?"

"What?"

"I took you into my home as if you were my own child and decided if no one wanted to love you, if the world wanted to spit at you, like they did at Christ, then *I* would love you, I would take care of you, feed you, change you, clean you."

"Thank you."

"But..."

"There's always a but..."

"I was not fit to be a parent. The Church was my whole life...it was all I ever knew. So, putting you into foster care, where you were abused, mocked and had your young heart turned to stone, was my mistake. For that I am sorry. When Charles Gaiman came to your foster home to discuss donating money, he saw you and got in contact with me to hear your whole story. Had I known what he'd do to you, then I would've never given him my blessing. I don't think it's a coincidence in the hands of a Jew you were perverted into this. It's my opinion that their kind has troubled this world for a very long time."

When he said that I stopped crying. I stopped feeling sorry for myself totally. Father Roger had shrunk in my eyes to the size of a shrew.

"You suddenly made me very proud of my heresy, Father. I might believe in orgies and drugs and ceremonial killing but...unlike you...I've never judged an entire group of people by their color or creed or the actions of their ancestors. This is why your God has been rejected, priest. This is why no one's buying your bull shit."

"Think what you will, you freak. You're not a man or woman, boy or girl, I don't respect your opinion. You're God's mistake. To your point, I've read up on all the religions, on Judaism and on Roman myth. So, I know who you claim to be and why you claim to be him. I also know you're not Bacchus or any deity of the sort. If that's who you think you are, I will do you the liberty of killing you appropriately."

"How do you plan on doing that?"

"Look out your window, child."

I followed Roger's pointing finger out the window to the foggy docks ahead of our vehicle.

"From water you came into this world and brought us winter. Now, demon, into water you shall return to welcome spring. It's only right."

The vehicle stopped and Merle turned off his engine and exited his car. Roger followed him out and opened my door, sticking his semen-white hand out to me.

"Take my hand, Danny."

I sensed the pervert desired my touch, so to tease him, I pulled open my robe and exposed myself to him.

"Vile creature," Roger spat.

I laughed and scooted down the seat and out of the car. I followed Roger and Merle toward the docks, where the wet wood beneath my feet soothed my skin and soul. We approached five burly men all dressed in black, standing by a boat called *Golgotha*.

"This is him. Make sure you don't throw him over until you're half an hour out," Merle instructed the men.

"Alright," one of the men in black nodded.

"This is as far as I can go. Think you can take care of it from here, Father?"

Roger nodded and Merle walked back down the docks and returned to his car. With him, all hope drove away.

The men unraveled a rope wrapped around a post and raised the boat's anchor back onto the deck. Once all the men boarded, they waited on Roger and me to get in.

"After you," Roger instructed me.

I took one big step into the boat and after having a bit of trouble, stood straight up on the deck. Roger needed the help of two of the men to get in. Now we were all securely onboard and the men started the engine and steered us forward. The sounds of the boat cruising through the still waters washed over any embers of sorrow or regret still smoldering inside me. I was prepared for my suffering to end. Part of me was already dead, one with Earth and cosmos anyway, just another lyric in the universe's song.

Inside the boat were two small rooms. One where the men would stay and another I shared with Roger. He pulled out a Bible and started softly reciting from it. By coincidence, the bobbing of the boat made me feel ill as soon as the book of Revelations reared its ugly head. I started vomiting everywhere.

Chapter Twenty-six
The Feeding Trough
Number Ten – The Chef

"While I was passing into death peacefully on one side of the city, on another, Jesus was having much more trouble accepting the inevitable. Inga, though, is more prepared than either of us. Inside she is celebrating but, on the outside, she must hide her enthusiasm in case it jinxes her chances of not getting out of this alive."
-Daniel Vaughn, Caretaker of The Collective

We were driving down a thin rural road with thick forests on either side of our van. I couldn't wait to be a part of the fresh soil just outside these walls. First, I'd have to be eaten, digested, and shit out. Which seems more and more possible seeing as the only place this van could be going is Gaiman farms where a vineyard, farm, and slaughterhouse are all in spitting distance. I sighed and looked up toward the Thief whose eyes were glued to the window, his mind was seemingly elsewhere.

"Jesus?"

He turned to me, curiously, "Yes, Inga?"

"Can I have your blessing?"

"My blessing?"

"Yes, I need your blessing to be eaten."

"What the hell are you talking about?"

"In ancient Greece, people would ask animals for consent when they wanted to be slaughtered. They would pour water onto the animal's head. If it shook off the water by nodding, the oracle would interpret this as the animal giving consent and would bless the butcher. The oracle would then say, "That which willing nods...I say you may justly sacrifice."

"You want to be eaten? Go the fuck ahead...there...you have my blessing."

"No, Jesus, you have to do this my way. My death won't feel right unless you do."

"Fine. No sweat off my sack."

I reached into my pocket and grabbed a half full water bottle to give to him, which he took with a frustrated expression.

"You've had water this whole time and didn't share?"

"I kept it with me just in case we'd be in this situation. Take just one sip if you must, but pour most of it onto my head."

I watched him suck out all the water in the bottle and with his mouth full, stood over me and spat it onto my head. I happily accepted his abuse and nodded, shaking the water off.

The Thief said to me, "That which willing nods...I say you may justly sacrifice."

"Thank you," I smiled.

The human privilege I'm born with makes me feel so guilty for how the pigs of Gaiman farms live and die. First, they herd them from their pens into a rubber chute that leads to the killing room floor. Each pig is then held in place by a mechanical monstrosity that restrains it while the "knocker," an employee wielding a stun gun, shoots the pig in the fucking head, knocking it out immediately. This process happens to every pig, one by one, on the disassembly line, so fast that abnormalities and diseases go unnoticed.

Once the pig is knocked out, it's hung up by its feet and stuck with a blade in the neck so it can bleed out. Thet then drained pig is dunked into a tank of scalding water to be purified. When the pig is hoisted out, it looks inorganic, somehow man-made. The carcass is now lowered onto a steel table where any remaining hair is removed with a scraper and *fucking* blowtorch. I remember the first time I read about this process on the internet and thought it was complete bull shit. When I was a young chef, we were taken on a tour of a factory farm and I got to see first-hand the sickening way my species prepares its food. That's when I knew I wanted to be martyred for this cause, if anything just to be a grain of rice on the other side of justice's scale.

If you think using a blowtorch on an animal that is exceptionally intelligent, carries ancestral memory, has more complex feelings than most mammals, and screams like a human child, is draconian, you should see these bastards take a power saw to a pig's pasty, white carcass running lengthwise, down the middle from the anus to the top of its head. The next step is for another employee to take out the animal's organs with their bare hands and sort them in a process that sends most of those organs into the trash.

These employees end their work days covered in blood and more sadistic than the day before. Behind closed doors, some of the acts of cruelty that have been reported are horrifying. Pregnant sows being bludgeoned with wrenches and having burning hot objects rammed into their rectums and vaginas. Cigarettes getting put out on them. Some are thrown into pits of pig shit to drown.

As the animal holocaust gravy train keeps on rolling, Jesus and I are on our way right into its heart, from which all the venom gets pumped into the world. If I'm lucky, my body will be cut in half and chopped up and mistaken for pork to wind up on some American family's dinner plate.

I broke apart from my manic world of violent delusion when our van finally arrived at the gate into the Gaiman Farms compound. The gate slowly crawled open and let us through, and we parked right in front of the slaughterhouse. After the two cops stepped out of the van, they strolled over to us and opened the back doors.

"Get out," one of the cops ordered.

Jesus and I stepped out of the van. The cops grabbed our arms and led us into the slaughterhouse. All of our senses were assaulted with the gross, visceral smell that shot up our noses, the soundscape of machinery, animal grunts, squeals, screams, and whimpers reaming our ears. The sight of corpses everywhere gave us the impression we were tourists in a death camp. The facility was filled with Mexicans hard at work, showing us neither mind nor shame in killing. Police Chief Merle Swanson was already there, standing atop a scaffold to watch over the facility.

"There you are...perfect timing, I got here only five minutes ago myself," Swanson said as he waved us over.

Once he got a good look at us, sizing up how much we suffered on our trip, he lifted up my chin with his finger.

"A little birdie told us you have always wished to be the one that is eaten, is this true?" Swanson asked me.

"Yes sir...please."

"Then you will get your wish...strip."

"Thank you," I said as I began to disrobe.

I took my shirt off, revealing my hormonally engineered breasts then dropped trou.

"Look at that little thing," Swanson guffawed at my penis.

The cops all started laughing and playfully punching each other in the ribs. Jesus lifted his head for the first time in a long while and stared at Swanson, smirking.

"What's the matter? Are you upset it's not bigger?" Jesus dared ask.

For this, Jesus immediately got Swanson's fist to his nose, almost breaking it.

"How fucking dare you? If it wasn't for protocol, I'd kill you right here and now."

The Thief was bent over, nursing his nose when he looked up at Swanson and bleeding, decided to twist the knife in Swanson's wound even further.

"Do it now while you have the chance, pig. Before you lose it," Jesus' nose blood trickled into his smile.

"I'll show you a pig," Swanson turned to his two lackey cops. "Take the tranny to the knocker."

The cops took my naked body back down the scaffold to the beginning of the disassembly line's rubber chute. Hopefully, somehow my blood and bones would clog or halt the machines and break this whole system down. The cops forced me down on all fours and walked me over to the knocker as the giant machine pressed its metal arms around me to keep me in place. The knocker walked up to me and pointed the stun gun an inch from my forehead and in the blink of an eye, I was out cold.

After that blink, I opened my eyes to discover I was hovering above my body, watching what would become of it. Shackles were attached to my feet and I was raised into the air, upside down to hang. Then a man came over with a knife and stabbed me in the jugular and jerked the knife across my throat. Thick globs of blood started pouring out of me. It felt like forever till all the blood in my body had been drained. Next, I was pulled down a zip-line over the scalding bath and dipped in. After a few minutes of this, I was pulled out and looked unrecognizable, like all my facial features had been ironed out. The zip-line then carried me over to two men, one to scrape my hair off, another to burn it off with the blowtorch. I was completely bald, bare, and alien when the zip-line pulled me over a table to be unshackled. I plopped onto the table and had a power saw driven through my body. Split in half, my brain was scooped out and thrown into the trash. Finally, my two halves were chopped up into numerous giblets.

I was hoping those pieces would be packaged like pork and thrown into the mix with the rest of the meat products, but to my dismay, instead the employees piled me into a wheel barrow and pushed me out of the slaughter house. My spirit followed them out and saw the employee take my body parts to the pig pens where they stopped at a long feeding trough. He then tipped over the wheel barrow and dropped my parts into the trough. The pigs were then released and had a feeding frenzy that devoured my flesh down to the bone. My life would amount to food for pigs which I suppose is only right. The perfect justice had been served. Hopefully, more people start volunteering for this. The one who must be eaten was me and without a real God to thank, I have to ask, *Why not Bacchus?*

Chapter Twenty-seven
Passing For A Pauper
Number Seven – The Thief

"With Jesus and I the only living Bacchae left, one of us must survive and the other must drown. So, no matter what happens, the future looks grim."
-Daniel Vaughn

Now that the Chef was dead, Swanson had me all to himself. We watched the Chef's body get cleaved to pieces from atop the scaffold. After they disposed of the body, Swanson turned to me with a giant grin on his face.

"Your turn."

He pointed down the scaffold and I started walking. He followed right behind me until we reached the floor.

"Take the door to your left," Swanson instructed me.

I walked through the door and the two other cops returned to Swanson's side. We stepped outside and walked around the pig pen where I could vaguely see the Chef's body being fed to the pigs. The vulgar, unmistakable smell of shit was in the air. Swanson sniffed twice.

"Did you shit your pants? Are you really that scared?" Swanson joked, making the other two cops laugh hysterically behind the handkerchiefs they were holding up to their noses.

Swanson led me to the manure lagoon that was connected to the pig pen. It was vast and deep and bubbling and brown. I couldn't help but spit up whatever rubbish was left in my stomach.

"The one that must be drowned," Swanson said.

"You can't be serious..." I replied.

"We don't have any other bodies of water around. Unless you want your head stuck in a toilet for an hour."

"That sounds much better."

"I was kidding."

I sighed, clearing my mind of any fear that would get in the way of me fighting for my life. Catching the bastards by surprise, I quickly bucked my shoulder into the chin of one cop behind me, knocking him unconscious, then punched the other, knocking him down but not out. That fallen cop grabbed my leg as I started wrestling with Swanson and the cop tipped us both over. With some kind of uncanny luck, I was able to pull Swanson forward so that he fell into the pig shit. Even though it was the shallow edge of the lagoon, Swanson was still in neck deep and covered. He screamed and splashed around, trying to get out. The other cop turned to Swanson but kept trying to subdue me.

"Don't let him escape," Swanson shouted as the cop held onto me, "Get me out of here first," Swanson shouted again as he sunk deeper, forcing the cop to run back and retrieve his boss.

I started running as fast as I could toward the vineyard. I was weak, dehydrated, exhausted, and delirious. I knew slowing down was equivalent to suicide. Once the cops pulled Swanson out of the shit, he ordered them to follow me. He ran like the wind but was too far behind me to see where I had hidden. I was hunkered down among the many rows of frozen grape vines where the farmers were tilling the soil through each row. One of the farmers discovered me hiding when I lifted my head off the ground to check if the coast was clear. That farmer started laughing.

"What are you doing?" he asked in our mother language.

"Hiding. Is he gone?"

"Your face..."

The farmer reached into his pocket and pulled out a handkerchief to throw down to me. I used it to wipe the blood from my nose while the farmer looked around and saw the cop running over, into the vineyard.

"You really think he's not going to find you?" the farmer looked back down at me and asked.

"There's gotta be some way you can help me," I begged, staring up at him, squinting as a beam of sunlight blared into my eyes.

"Get up, I have an idea," the farmer said.

I stood up and together we crept over to a tractor and I hopped on as he took the steering wheel. We drove out of the vineyard to a nearby cabin.

"What is your name?" the farmer asked.

"Jesus... and you are?"

"Enrique," he told me before shaking hands.

"Where are you taking me, Enrique?" I asked.

"Our barracks."

Enrique parked the tractor and we climbed off and ran into the barracks. Inside the darkened living quarters were multiple bunk beds and closets for each of the farmers.

"Why was that policeman chasing you?"

"It's a long story but I did nothing wrong. I didn't hurt anyone. You have to believe me, I'm one of you, born and raised in Guadalajara."

"I believe you," Enrique nodded.

"They won't leave this farm until they find me. I have to hide."

"The best way to hide is in plain sight. Come."

Enrique grabbed my hand and took me to his bunk. He sat down and opened up his nightstand where he pulled out some barbershop clippers.

"I don't understand."

"They won't find you if they can't recognize you."

Enrique plugged in his clippers and they began buzzing, hungry for my scalp.

"Sit."

Enrique pushed me down, pulled my hair back and started shaved my head from the top, back. Long strands of my raven locks fell to the floor, and by the end of my haircut, I looked more like the farmers than I did myself. Enrique went on to find me some clothes to wear and once I changed, I stood in front of the mirror to examine myself.

"You're almost there...just one more thing."

"Enrique walked over to a different bunk and glanced around the room to make sure no one was looking. He then opened up another farmer's cabinet and stole an eyepatch from it. He walked over to me and strapped the eyepatch on my face, over my left eye. It blurred my vision and made it difficult to orient my distance from objects but still, Swanson wouldn't be able to pick me out of a lineup.

"You ever worked on a farm before?" Enrique asked.

"Yes. A long time ago."

We left the barracks and strolled back to the tractor without trying to hide ourselves. In plain sight, we drove through the vineyard. We saw Swanson and his two lackeys creeping through the vineyard searching high and low for me. I even waved and smiled at them. Still, they had no clue.

Swanson and his men left dejected and kicking up the soil in disgrace. I would survive, today.

The police raided the farm everyday over the next week and would walk inches from my face in search of me. Even though my life was in peril there, I found a certain level of comfort on this farm and among other people who looked like me. This is where I'd spend the next few months, waiting for my hair and the grapes to grow. At first, the work felt like a betrayal of all the values I used to hold. Like I should've been elsewhere, drinking the marrow out of life, living a real experience, not working for any bosses, spending my time writing poems because after all, these hands of mine are a poet's hands no matter how much earth they tend. It was as if I avoided hard labor like this for so long in favor of an artist's life that it was finally my time to eat my fair share of the shit and after not having to work for so long, shit tasted delicious.

After my hands developed numerous callouses and my brown skin turned a darker hue and after learning about all the effort that goes into making the perfect wine, I came to understand hard work was the real marrow to suck out of life. The real poetry was in being like everyone else, sweating and bleeding to share in the creation of something to give the rest of the world. I was no longer a starving poet. Now every bite of meat and sip of wine contained new hints of flavor only accessible to those that earned their stake.

When the sun would set and our work was finished, nightfall would treat us to the delights meant only for those who broke their backs during the day. The stars would blink and sparkle in the rhythm of my heart. My soul would crackle like a campfire, gloriously burning in the darkness, untouchable and grateful to the universe that gave me new purpose. The poetry in my mind faded and became the poetry of my hands. I felt like freshly tilled soil, knowing I could grow grapes sweeter than any you've ever tasted.

Chapter Twenty-eight
The Last Bacchae
Number One – The Hierophant – Hersh

"I could sense a sharp tranquility. I knew exactly what it must be. My lucky Number Seven had gotten away. I didn't need an oracle to tell me he survived, all I needed was a certain twinkle in the stars. Jesus Madrid lived through the Bacchus Death Collective and came out nobler on the other side. I love you, Jesus, you've always been an inspiration to me."
-Danny Vaughn

I had just vomited, making Roger stop reciting scripture and look up from his Bible at me, frustrated.

"Are you going to clean that up?"

"I'm used to having someone do it for me."

He shook his head, stood up, then walked over to the bathroom. He grabbed a towel and set it in the sink to let the water run over it. Once it was damp enough, Roger pulled the towel out and threw it at me.

"Clean it or I'll have to call in the others."

"Go ahead. Do your worst," I dared him. "Let's see what you're really made of, priest."

Roger sighed and walked to the door, "Fine but I warned you."

Roger left the room and closed the door behind him. He was gone for only a minute when he reopened the door and stepped in with the other five men, all thrilled to punish me.

"What are you going to do?" I challenged the lot. "Spank me?"

"Get on your knees," Roger ordered.

I laughed and spread my legs to show the other men my curious privates.

"What the fuck is that?" one of the men asked, shocked.

"Disgusting," another man spat.

"So, is it a boy or girl?" the third simpleton asked.

"They're neither and both at the same time, they're a very special child," Roger replied.

"It ain't special," the final, fifth man shrugged and approached me, unimpressed.

With one hand, he grabbed my undeveloped penis and tugged it to its full length.

I smiled, deviously, "That's it, now stroke it up and down."

With his free hand, he reached into his pocket and pulled out something he hid in his closed fist. When he brought it closer to my penis and pressed a button on the object, a blade popped out. I didn't register what was coming in time to scream or squirm, and with one quick cut, he completely removed the appendage. My thighs immediately clamped shut as blood started gushing all over my crotch, thighs, and legs. I looked down and saw my member on the ground, completely coated in red and although it lay still, it seemed as though it could flinch or spasm at any moment. It was only then that my eyes grew wide and I started screaming, terribly.

"Now she's a girl," the butcher laughed at his own j but the humor was lost in the horror of my bloody shrieking.

"Dude, the kid's fucking bleeding everywhere," one of the men fretted.

"Who gives a fuck? We gotta throw him over right about now anyway."

"What the fuck are we waiting for?"

"I don't know, let's go."

"Hear that, kid? You won't have to suffer for long."

I kept screaming, in too much pain and shock to even hear what anyone said. With mercy, one man punched me clean in the mouth, knocking me out.

"Oh my, this has got me so excited," squealed Roger happily, rubbing his hands together and licking his lips.

As everyone piled out of the room, one of the men carried my bleeding body over his shoulder, getting his chest covered in my blood. They brought me out on the deck and laid me down by the rail to wrap the anchor's chain around my legs. Once the anchor was secured to me, he slapped me awake until the pain came flooding back into me all over again. I spit up more vomit and looked up to see all my killers looking down at this mess they've created.

"My body will die but my spirit will go on. More people will drink, dance, and fuck than ever. The spell of control your God has cast on the world has finally been lifted. The next two thousand years belong to Bacchus. What you know as sanity will be considered madness and what you know as madness will be considered sanity. Bacchus-Christ, Christ-Bacchus, life-death, it's all the same, so just go on and kill me already."

Roger spit directly in my face.

"Go back to the watery hell you came from, demon. You're not a god at all," Roger turned to each of the men. "Go on, throw it over."

The strongest of the men lifted me up with the anchor and walked me to the edge of the boat. He then raised me over his head and threw me into the freezing ocean. The salt water burned my wound as it sucked me under. I didn't bother trying to fight for air, in fact, I swam down with the anchor, watching the light that was hitting the ocean's surface disappear until everything went black. Soon, my lungs filled with water and I lost consciousness. True black. I sensed my brain die and spirit pass and then that spirit shot up out of the sea toward the same heavens that Roger had raised his hands up to.

"Praise Jesus," he shouted.

Epilogue
Number Seven – The Thief

"On the other side of living, Hades greets me fondly. I meet all my old friends. Charles, Opal, Sal, even the Musician is here playing accordion. This place is filled with music, dance, sex and wine. I don't know why you people put up such a fight trying to avoid it."
-Daniel Vaughn, a God Even in Hell

Life on Gaiman Farms only lasted six months. When the warmer months arrived, I met a French woman there, touring the country in search of the best wines, right from their vineyards. She left with a few bottles of red and me in tow, drunkenly banging her at every stop until I made a few forgeries and got myself on her plane back to Paris. It was my first time stepping foot onto European soil. Imagine that, a poor Mexican boy like me, walking across the same cobblestones that all the great poets once graced.

After a few weeks of my Frenchy showing me the country, fucking her inside out, I became bored with her, France and the French. After, I decided to go my own way. I hopped between borders, getting drunk in the country sides and high in the metropolitan whore houses. Everywhere I went was my own private red light district. Most people thought I was an Arab, so I picked up a few words and played the part when it came in handy. I stayed with families from every region of every country, they took me in like one of their own and showed me how they lived.

After a few months of this, my hands turned soft and supple again, as a poet's should be. The lyrical flow that vanished when I started working on the farm reappeared to guide me on my leisurely sunset strolls. I started writing those verses down as soon as they came to me. By now I have more than two hundred poems, all ready to be published if I can find someone willing to finance the cost of printing, distribution, and marketing. I need to find a rich man, perhaps that'll be my wish upon the next shooting star I see. The same way I wished to meet the owner of America and was drawn to Charles Gaiman, I'll have to wish to meet the owner of Europe. I decided it would be best to search for him in Switzerland. I hear they have quite a lot of bankers.

About the Author

Robert Shepyer is a writer that blends the macabre and humorous in a way that will make you laugh so hard that you will squirt black milk out of your nose. With a tone that marries adult nightmares with children's cartoons, he tries to soften the suffering he sees in the world by translating it into a caricature of its worst self.

Also by the Author
at
Rogue Phoenix Press

Low Key

Low Key is the story of Los Angeles detective and Marfan syndrome sufferer, Illy Robin. In 2025, after the self-driving car has revolutionized transportation and forced thousands into homelessness, Illy is hired by billionaire real estate tycoon Randolph Royce to find his daughter, Dorothy. As a reward, Royce sets Illy on a string of blind dates but every girl winds up dead the next day after the date. Suspected by police for his involvement, Illy must clear his name and find the real killer. Perverting the archetypes of our childhood-favorite animated films, Illy sees every girl that he fancies as a different Princess, showing us the raw streets of Los Angeles through "Disneyfied" eyes.

Chapter One
The Imaginary Man

After she read my words, she couldn't love me. If that was how my mind ticked then she must've married the wrong cat. I tried to tell her I was from a different age but she wasn't having it, nothing could excuse my complete lack of literary talent and she would rather be alone than love a hack. Before she left the last time, her parting words to me were, *"Keep it low key"*.

In my Disneyfied mind, Maria mistook me for the perfect Beast to her Belle. The only problem was that Beast was rich and I was poor and Belle loved books while Maria loved film. In actuality, I was more like Quasimodo, which would make sense because Esmeralda never really loved him back.

That's unfair though. There was a time when we loved each other so obsessively I could look at her one certain way and her whole pale body would blush bright pink before melting in my arms. Conversely, Maria was the skeleton key to my mind, body, and soul. Only once she unlocked those trinkets and spent some time inside them, she grew bored with me.

I cannot stress this enough; quantity of pain endured has no relation to quality of love dispensed. That's what our marriage taught us after three years. Maria thought I, Illy Robin, had been through so much pain I was tenderized to the point I could love more deeply than any other. The truth was pain never gave me anything but the ability to endure more pain.

For every decade of my life there's been a different disease or disorder. I was born with Marfan syndrome, a disorder that expresses itself as extremely as the disfiguring wretchedness of the Elephant Man or as subtly cool as the spindly limbed Joey Ramone. Thankfully, I resemble the latter, on the outside.

At five, I was stricken with Idiopathic Thrombocytopenic Purpura. I spent my formative years between babyhood and kidhood in Children's hospital, spotted up and down with brown and purple bruises. All of us damaged goods would sleep in one big quarantine with Disney movies playing through the night on a closed-circuit TV. We neither watched nor slept, we would lie back, stare up at the ceiling and wait for God to answer, "What will become of us?"

By the time I was shipped off to school, I already had an intimate relationship with death. Antisocial and mutated by puberty, I was bullied every day and toughened up to prepare myself for a career in evasion, de-escalation, and sneak. I became a private detective. A dick. Funny thing is, my bully got into investigation too, only he ended up bullying on behalf of the LAPD. There was a time when being a private eye in LA was considered cliché but now, in 2025, it's an anachronism. You'll know it's a police state when there are no more P.I.'s. And yeah, maybe I romanticize my career, getting tattoos of Sam Spade, Phillip Marlowe, and Lew Archer on my stomach and naming my gun Beretta James...

"When she sings, she don't go *bang, bang, bang*... she go *scat, scat, scat*."

I figure romanticizing gives this lonely beat some purpose.

Maria was the last woman who made love to me and that was three years ago. I've found living without the therapy of sex makes the mind question the reality of every object. I'll jay-walk through a busy street, see a car coming, and stare at the only passenger in the back seat as if daring him to exist. Will this car actually hit me? No, they're not designed to do that, nothing is anymore.

This feeling that envelopes me, this detachment...I cannot pursue the act of love when I am arrested in the condition of love. I feel like an imaginary person...that somehow animated himself.

Chapter Two
Briefly, on Vermin Culture

History consolidates the noteworthy into three categories; heroes, villains, and victims. The hero culture in our movies is in stark contrast to the victim culture of our people. This victim culture was created by the villain class to desensitize and deprive us of the skills we need to serve the modern machine. They are teaching us to fear love because people that don't love don't reproduce.

I imagine the energies collected from all our missed opportunities to seize the moment and kiss the girl have been combining and multiplying into the black hole that will eat the world. All the love that never was is churning, colliding, sucking, and collapsing forever into impotent nothing.

To the villains we were never victims, we were vermin. Ain't it just like the rich to protect the evil that did them good?

FOR THE FULL INVENTORY
OF QUALITY BOOKS:
http://www.roguephoenixpress.com

Rogue Phoenix Press
Representing Excellence in Publishing

**Quality trade paperbacks and downloads
in multiple formats,
in genres ranging from historical to contemporary romance, mystery
and science fiction.
Visit the website then bookmark it.
We add new titles each month!**

www.ingramcontent.com/pod-product-compliance
Lightning Source LLC
Chambersburg PA
CBHW060430130626
46555CB00005B/2286